Inevitably, each life must contend with serious—even dangerous—undertows.
Sometimes the pull is literal; sometimes it's metaphorical.
Sometimes it's both.

   Her headache a whirlpool of complaint, Cassie picked her way through fallen branches to the bluff. The dry clifftop grasses clung together, rustled nervously. The ocean was heavy with graywhite swells.
   Cassie stumbled onto the rocks. Something rough and spiky pushed hard, cut through her left sandal. She felt sticky moistness trickle along her foot.
   She could see the spreading upspray, jeweled by long remnants of sunlight. Slowly she squished to the blowhole, going close. Closer. Closer still. Spray blew into her face, stinging, coarse. Icy.
   At the edge, she peered down. A trick of reflection splayed light fragments throughout the shaft. Jagged stone knuckles dripped. Ebony scarfaces seeped.
   Far below, past brutal stalactites and oozing sidespikes, the impatient surf frothed, heaved, sought freedom.
   Then it pulsed, lurched, reared...

from "Undertow", one of the 18 compelling stories in this new anthology.

UNDERTOW

Stories

Eric E. Wallace

Rabbit Creek Creative
Anchorage, Alaska - Eagle, Idaho

Copyright © 2014 by Eric E. Wallace

ISBN 978-1-63263-280-7

All rights reserved. No part of this publication may be reproduced, stored in a retrieval system, or transmitted in any form or by any means, electronic, mechanical, recording or otherwise, without the prior written permission of the author.

Published by BookLocker.com, Inc., Bradenton, Florida.

Cover photography: © Mossel_Dreamstime.com

The characters and events in this book are fictitious. Any similarity to real persons, living or dead, is coincidental and not intended by the author.

Some stories in this collection have appeared elsewhere, some in slightly different form. The author gratefully acknowledges these periodicals, anthologies and organizations:

Toasted Cheese Literary Journal: "Cell Block"
Rosebud Magazine: "Under the Hood"
The First Line: "Loch Ness Monsters"
Writers in the Attic—Rooms: "Birds of Prey" & "Room Enough"
Writers in the Attic—Detours: "Road Work"
WritersWeekly.com: "Long Road Home" & "In the Moment"
Petaluma Readers Theater: "Undertow"

Printed in the United States of America on acid-free paper.

First Edition

Rabbit Creek Creative
2014

In loving memory of

LINDA SUTHERLAND

and

IAN WALLACE

For Kathy

Contents

Jericho 1
Meter Running 17
Room Enough 37
Under the Hood 43
In the Moment 63
Charley Horse 69
Cell Block 77
Loch Ness Monsters 89
Road Work 111
Shades of Gray 119
Long Road Home 129
Maestro 133
Undertow 175
Birds of Prey 181
Playing Doctor 187
Late 211
Spoons 215
Beneath 219

Acknowledgements 233
About the Author 235

Jericho

"So, there I was having coffee with Joe Hazelwood, The Man himself." Jericho liked telling this story.

"Who?"

"Captain Joseph Hazelwood, skipper of the Exxon Valdez."

This got another puzzled reaction.

'C'mon, Shrug. You know—the oil tanker that went aground in Alaska, screwed up the environment. A million dead birds, poached in oil. Remember?'

"Huh."

Jeez, thought Jericho. When you make friends in a shelter you sure take your chances on the level of smarts. Despite the white eyebrows and wild, cottony hair, Shrug was no Einstein.

Unleashing one of his many complicated shoulder twitches, Shrug hunched further into his shell. So much for a willing ear.

As usual, the place reeked of disinfectant. Jericho stared moodily at the coffee rings on the sticky tablecloth. They looked like the Audi logo. He'd love to have an Audi. He'd love to have any car. He hadn't driven in, how many years? Not since he came back to Boise. Not since he drove that clunker of a taxi in Alaska, skidding around on the icy streets, scaring his passengers. God, that was some driving!

He drained his coffee and smudged the four rings with his empty mug. No more German car, just an ugly brown smear.

That reminded him. He had to get out of there before they tabbed him for KP. Or worse, forced him go practice for the choir they were trying to set up.

The Jesus Joint—his private term for the mission—was a necessary evil in Jericho's life. Well, maybe not evil, but they got very pushy with all the religious stuff. We help your body, you give us your soul. Jericho was good at dissembling, and put out just enough repentant shuck and jive to convince everyone he was a humble sinner, ready to be led by his nose to salvation.

In fact, growing up, he'd been deluged with tons of holy moly claptrap and biblical nonsense by his fanatical mother and his belt-wielding father, and although he'd fled the whole sorry family scene in his teens, his stubborn and quirky mind hung on to the sour, sanctimonious aftertaste, chapter and verse. So when he showed up at the Jesus Joint for a meal or a bed, he knew how to brownnose them lock, stock and scripture.

Behind their backs, Jericho had his fun. When he was roped into choir practice, he'd sing slightly off-pitch, throwing the inexperienced singers beside him into broken falsettos and trembling dissonance. He also liked changing the words he sang to confuse casual listeners. 'Jesus loves me, this is snow.' 'Onward, Christian boulders.' 'Cherish the old rugged corpse.' Small pleasures.

He'd shuffle through the food line—the shuffling also an act—inwardly smiling at his private names for the grub. He'd try to keep a straight face as the volunteers dished up Meatloaf ala Matthew, Jehovah's

Jericho

Jell-O, Divine Dumplings or, his favorite, The Holy Ghost on Toast, Which was a helluva lot better, he thought, than the name vets used for creamed chipped beef, Shit on a Shingle.

"Well, Gerald," the director would beam at him. "What are you going to do with your life?" Jericho thought Mr. Gunnison had the bright-eyed fervor of a recovering alky or a bornagain ex-con. Or maybe both.

"Isn't that God's business? My life, I mean." Give them their own medicine.

Gunnison was up to the task. "Not totally God's business, no. It's more a partnership. He gives you the opportunities, but you have to act on them."

"So God's sort of like a CEO?"

"Come on, now, Gerald, you know what I mean." The ever-brilliant smile was upstaged by puffs of oily garlic. Tuning out, Jericho studied a picture of Jesus commanding the wall. Wasn't there once a drummer in a Garden City band who looked just like that? Maybe Jesus had been sitting in? He sure played a heckuva riff.

Even before he was dismissed, Jericho was thinking again about his trumpet, an old battered silver Bach with a secret sweet voice. He needed to scrape up some cash to get it out of hock. Someone might actually buy the thing, and then where'd he be? It was his teddy bear, his security blanket and his lucky charm all rolled into one. Time was when he'd been pretty good on that horn. These days, when he only played it in deserted lots and back alleys, trying to keep his chops in shape, something was missing.

Eric E. Wallace

You don't pawn Miles or Dizzy or Wynton. But you sure pawn Jericho aka Gerald, the former whiz kid, bright future and all that, whose circuits blew out from genetic fluke, synaptic hernia, fratboy acid-dropping, one head smack too many from the Gipper, who knows? At any rate, Jericho's once-dazzling trumpet was in and out of pawn shops like they had revolving doors. He had to get it back again.

Jericho went out into the hot bright Boise day, shouldered past the usual strays and stragglers, and strode towards the nearest park, already thinking, planning.

He had two pressing needs, and both involved money. He wanted his goddam trumpet back, just because. And he wanted a ticket to that concert tonight at the Egyptian. He'd learned his son Robbie was playing, the little bastard he hadn't seen since Robbie was maybe four months old. Jericho didn't think he cared if he actually met the kid, but he was intrigued by what he'd learned about him. Which was, if you believed Iris and her fatass friends, that Robbie was gifted in a big musical way. A pianist with a future, she'd said. Beats being a penis with no future, he'd quipped. Iris wasn't amused. Their son had turned out good, she said, maybe great. You shoulda stuck around.

Reconnecting with Iris was never one of Jericho' goals. He'd been back in Boise almost a year before he bumped into her. She was coming off shift at a bakery where he was scrounging free day-olds. Iris still had the face of an angel, but now that face was driving a tank of

Jericho

a body. He couldn't believe they'd done the hot and heavy back in the day. He didn't like fat, not one bit. Double glad he went on the lam. But what the heck, when Iris invited, he joined her for a cup of coffee, her treat, and listened to twenty years of kid-raising stories, with occasional little jabs chucked in. Highly-charged phrases, like 'deserted us', 'ought to have married' and 'escaped to Alaska' only showed up a few times.

"So you make something of yourself in Anchorage?" Iris asked, fluffing out her dough-stained uniform. She smelled of ginger and cleanser. Not a good mix.

For some reason Jericho decided to be truthful. "Look, the oil company gig didn't last. Drove a cab for a time. Did some janitorial. Got down on my luck, had to hit the streets once or twice. Wasn't bad, except for the winters. Finally couldn't take them. But interesting times. And hey, I even got to hobnob with Captain Hazelwood. How about that?"

"Who?"

"The guy who sailed his oil tanker into a reef, caused that humongous spill."

"Oh, yeah, him. Shit, Jerry, you trying to be a sailor too? Or are you just some kind of shipwreck?" Iris still knew how to zing them. And that hit close to the bone. He'd often thought how he and Hazelwood had screwed up their lives, both gone adrift. Both on the rocks.

In the old days, he'd have decked Iris. But that wasn't the best idea in the middle of a Moxie Java. He sipped his coffee, suppressed the anger. "Naw, Hazelwood was doing community service at the shelter.

We schlepped boxes together, got to talk about this and that. Nice guy, considering."

"So why are you fucking around with this homeless shit, Jerry? You still got a brain, doncha? College guy. Pretty fair musician as I recall. And you still got looks." Iris softened, and the old come-hither summons peeked out, plain as day.

"I'm not homeless. Not really. Think of me as a professional of the streets."

Iris snickered. "God, a panhandler by any other name..."

Am I a panhandler? Jericho thought now, watching a honking flock of geese invade the park. God, maybe. But it was temporary. Had to be. At the moment he simply didn't have focus, that's all. Could have been a fine history teacher. Used to be a damn good horn player. And he was the best fucking cabbie in Boise. He had a migrating bird's sense of direction, knew every street and back alley better than Santa Claus. Same thing driving a taxi in Anchorage, despite the wacky one-way streets. But in both cities he'd run afoul of his quick temper and his smart mouth. He still remembered the angry firings, the blown second chances. Even when you get used to it, the old heave-ho hurts.

As he sat in the park, Jericho could have been taken for an office worker on a break. He kept his clothes passably respectable, and he took pains to shave no matter what. He still had the lanky good looks of Clint Eastwood in his prime, still had an unravaged face and deceptively gentle eyes. He could radiate kindness and

Jericho

meekness, even when he felt neither. Very useful for a street professional. I guess I'm blessed. Blessed? Ain't that ironic?

So, cash? he mused. Borrow from Iris? Nope, fat chance, in both senses, although if Iris believed he needed money to hear Robbie play that might soften her up. But there'd be strings.

Iris had more strings than a piano. Steal a bike, use the library's computers, sell it on Craig's list? That had worked before, but he guessed the cops and the cyclists were getting wise.

He didn't have the time to stand around on busy corners, pleading his case with hand-lettered cardboard, though once in a while that produced a bigtime guilt-ridden sucker. He remembered one fat cat in a black Caddy who powered down those sleek tinted windows and forked over a hundred bucks, plus a free whiff of hotshot cologne and a gust of cool air conditioning. But Jericho couldn't count on that kind of payday. It would have to be the old hard-luck story routine, something he tried not to use too often. Boise's still a pretty small town. You get to be recognized.

Jericho reviewed his tales. Lost wallet, dying sister, need a bus ticket to Twin, uninsured girlfriend in hospital, lost backpack, stolen bicycle with all my possessions aboard. True story. Except he was the one swiping the bike and its goodies. Easy pickings.

That made him think about OneTooth Bill, riding his five and dime bike all over Anchorage, even in winter, carrying everything he owned and wearing every damn stitch of clothing he had, bulked up so huge he was like the Michelin Tire character, only in grungy orange. Bill's outfit looked like a prison jump suit—which maybe it was—and its color alerted drivers as he pedaled along like a hermit crab on wheels, flashing his one-tooth greeting.

God, the people you meet at the shelter. Take Alaska Max, forever stooped forward in deepest thought, walking hundreds and hundreds of miles of downtown Anchorage streets in any weather, his long white hair cascading about him. And the remarkable thing, Jericho had learned from a fare, an indiscrete attorney, was that Alaska Max had a huge trust fund sitting there for the asking, but he refused to touch it. Max just kept walking and thinking, year after year. The supreme street person.

Boise's shelters had their share of characters. Jericho's small circle had some beauts. There was the short and scrappy Luther, a perpetual wisecracker who'd rechristened Jerry when he'd foolishly shown his trumpet. The name Jericho stuck. There was UpWind Sally, master of the one-cheek fart, Blinky, whose huge eyes were always open and staring at nothing, and the redoubtable Shrug, rumored to be a former pro tight end who faked out defenders with his expressive shoulders. Jericho had grown fond of them, but not one could help with his cash flow. He needed to start now, find a few prospects and hope for a little luck.

He knew the lay of the land intimately and chose his hunting locations with skill. He likened himself to the generals he'd studied in history class, strategizing, outthinking, outflanking.

Jericho

He scored first, if modestly, outside an upscale office building, his worn but kind face supporting a tale of need. This one was about a friend fighting cancer. He varied the story near government offices where the salaries were good and the workers not so full of themselves as to look down on him. But so far the returns were middling. The crummy economic times pinched his profession also.

As he stood deferentially in a parking lot, pitching a story of lost luggage and a missing wallet to a nervous woman, real tears drifted down his cheek, and he realized, shit, I'm a method actor. All I gotta do is think of the fucked-up years, and it makes everything more believable. God yes, a method actor. A method street pro. He asked for a few dollars, and the woman, sniffling, gave him twice as much and wished him well.

In Anchorage, where he'd first panhandled, he'd learned the trick of sometimes asking for a specific, odd amount, like $16.23—'that's all I'm short for my train ticket back to Fairbanks'—and of course they'd round it up to twenty bucks. Sometimes he'd ask for a business card so he could 'return the loan'. That often clinched the deal.

But today, despite turning it on full bore, Jericho was coming up short. He realized he might not make his goal. And that's when he surprised himself. He'd pinpointed a man near the courthouse, where you gotta weed 'em out carefully, avoiding the billable hours types and the plainclothes detectives. This guy looked well-heeled and not in a big rush. Jericho, wanting a few tears to practice his method acting, thought of the education and talent he'd squandered, the son he'd rejected, the waste of it all, and then suddenly floored himself by being totally honest. He told the man about his screwed-up life, his unfocused yearnings, his desire to hear his son play the piano. No self-pity, only the facts, human error and human need. And the truth worked. The man, moved, handed him the amount for the concert, plus a few bucks. Now Jericho had enough for the ticket and the trumpet, with some left over.

It was a long, sweaty hike to the pawnshop, but he hoofed it there in record time. The pawnbroker, a lean, sallow frowner with crafty eyes, examined the grubby receipt and the cash, rummaged around, and finally produced the trumpet, dusty but safe. Jericho stood there, holding his beloved Bach like a newborn.
Thank god the guy wasn't so smart as to figure out the real value.
"Anything else, buddy?" asked the pawnbroker, his voice like a cracked tuba. He'd traded with Jericho before. That shabby trumpet would be back.
"Naw, I've got a concert to get to." Jericho left the cluttered store. Concert? That sounded pretty good. Let the guy think I'm blowing my horn with the Boise Phil tonight. Well, maybe in some sleaze bar. Well, shit.
Jericho walked to the mission and scrounged a shower in exchange for an hour in the kitchen. Big Lefty, grumbling, set him to peeling potatoes, something he didn't mind. He scraped away, poking out mealy eyes, thinking about skipping tonight's Moses Meatballs

Jericho

and treating himself to a real hamburger. Jesus wants me for a sunspot, he hummed.

He showered, shaved, carefully spruced himself up. On the way out he had to pass through a gantlet of banter from the regulars. "Hot date tonight, Jericho?" "Hey, what's that smell—clean?" "Call you a cab, boss?" He waved at UpWind Sally as she farted her way in to dinner. Tonight he loved them all.

The burger tasted great, but nervousness churned Jericho's stomach. Something down there flailed about like seabirds trapped in black crude. Shoving aside the rest of the fries, he shouldered his backpack, left the diner and walked uptown to the Egyptian. Thank god there were still plenty of seats. He'd not thought about that. A sellout would have been a killer.

But now came a shock. This wasn't a jazz combo or some big band show. This was Robbie all alone. A solo concert. Iris might have said something, but he'd missed it while ducking her mixed signals. Christ, just Robbie and the piano. And Robbie's own music, improvising. All his kid. Goddamn amazing.

Jericho found a seat in the third row, slightly off-center, ideal for watching Robbie play. He'd almost chosen the very front but developed cold feet. Even if Robbie could see the audience, there was no way he'd recognize his old man. Hell, Iris said she'd burned what few photos there were from back then. But Jericho was getting very nervous about it all.

He looked at the single-sheet program. Not even a photo. Only a few sentences about the concert and how Robbie would improvise this music on the spot, likely a mix of styles. Christ, that takes guts. Did his kid have guts? Who'da thought? And the bio was brief. Jeez, Robbie had graduated from UW, now lived in Seattle. Who knew? No mention of parents. Why should there be? But damn! Credit where credit's due! What about those good genes?

As the audience straggled in, Jericho studied the faux Egyptian décor, the gilded columns, swans and scarabs, bare-breasted maidens, aloof gods and goddesses. They'd all inhabited this old theater since it was a movie house. He remembered sitting up in the dark balcony as a teenager, Newman or Redford seducing his dates, making them more receptive to his exploring hands. Jeez, this place still smelled of popcorn.

It was almost time. The theater was only half full. Jericho felt annoyed, offended. He had an urge to jump up and demand more people. This was his kid. He knew the disappointment of playing to sparse crowds. There'd been too many nights when he'd sat in with half-ass bands in half-ass lounges, played his heart out, hit top notes so pure everyone's hair shot straight up, then saw how few creeps were sitting there, most of them getting drunk, caring less. No wonder everything went down the shitter.

The house lights dimmed and spots came up on the grand piano. Jericho's heart lurched. Jeez, it's like stage fright. Can you believe it? I got stage fright. And out came Robbie, dressed casually in black. Tall, good looking guy, Jericho's trim build, Iris' appealing face, long dark hair. Pride, guilt and sadness surged over Jericho. All those years, gone.

Robbie nodded at the applause, sat on the bench, breathed deeply, and began to play.

From the first arpeggio, Jericho was hooked. He untensed, settled back. Robbie explored the keyboard like a master, teasing with unpredictable chord progressions, challenging with unusual key changes, turning dissonance into joyful surprise, interweaving melodies of grace and beauty. This was no New Age noodling. It was classical yet not, jazz but much more. Christ, this kid, his kid, was better than Keith Jarrett in his heyday.

The improvisations soon took Jericho far away. He closed his eyes and was swept through all the years he'd missed, the brightness his life could have been.

The first piece ended, too soon, to robust applause, Jericho among the most enthusiastic. Robbie sat for a moment then began playing again. He performed three more extended improvisations, each taking Jericho deep into himself, his memories, his longings. The last piece was the most complex, harmonically rich, melodically captivating, rhythmically intriguing. The beauty and originality overwhelmed Jericho. He felt inspired by his connection to it all, however tenuous. At times he almost believed he'd left his body and was pouring his own soul through the keys, hammers, and strings, resonating magic into the hall, feeling the creative force pulse through him. How could a young guy like Robbie understand so much of love, of grief, of life?

The music moved into a final huge jazzy romp across the keyboard, and Jericho came to. He had the urge to leap up and play along, letting his silver horn soar with unconstrained delight above the wild ocean of chords. His hand dropped to the backpack and touched his trumpet through the cloth before he caught himself and sat back again, heart pounding.

As the last incredible notes faded, in the sudden, stunned silence before the audience roared and scrambled to its feet, he wanted to jump up and shout, "This is my son, isn't he great? This is my son!' Instead, he slumped there, breathless.

After the prolonged applause, people pushed toward the stage, surrounding an exhausted Robbie. Iris had shown up from somewhere. She stood proudly near the piano, slowly fanning herself with a program. Jericho, still in the third row, hesitated. He wanted to go up, to congratulate his son, at the very least to shake his hand. He took the backpack and moved toward the aisle, but things began to play in his head. *Hi, remember me? I'm your long-lost father, the jerk who didn't stick around, ran off to Alaska, never got in touch, never got his head together, but you'll understand and we'll connect, and did you know I used to play the trumpet pretty good and we'll turn my life around?* He couldn't. Not now. Jericho reached the aisle, took a last look at his son, and walked slowly out of the theater.

It was another sweltering desert evening. He wanted to think. He wandered down the boulevard, through stale cigar smoke, dodging boisterous bar goers. The

Jericho

lights of the old train depot beckoned from the hill ahead. A final shard of sunset edged a lone cloud with red.

Jericho made his way down to one of the town's oldest parks, followed a curving road toward the river and stood on the shadowy bank. He listened to the swiftly-flowing water. Sometimes the river made music for him. Not tonight. He crossed the road and walked over the lumpy grass to the old band shell. Bent completely in on themselves, a last pair of lovers strolled past him. No one else was around.

The band shell was nothing fancy. A tile roof, high, stucco walls, a large open arch. Jericho climbed on to the long stage. A lone beetle scurried away, hunched like Shrug. *Sorry, friend.* The night was deepening rapidly, and the first stars made tentative appearances above the trees. Jericho removed his trumpet from the backpack, pulled out a clean t-shirt and carefully dusted the instrument.

He knew the cops would eventually come by, ready to roust anyone hanging around the park after dark. Tonight, he thought, they might be in for a treat. At least for a surprise. Standing stage center, he made vigorous raspberries with his lips, jiggled the valves, raised the instrument, buzzed into the mouthpiece.

The first scratchy notes were awful. He winced. The next sounds were dreadful, nearly screeches.

For a time, it didn't get much better. But he kept at it, shaping, smoothing, searching for his old easy style.

At last it started to come back. He let loose with his own distinctive growl, wailing deep into the darkening sky—keen tones, jagged runs, edgy glissandos, wild staccato leaps, and daring, imperfect trills.

He thought of his son at the piano, immersed in creative ecstasy, and he slowed, softened, began to blow loss and pain and longing into the horn.

And as night settled in, Jericho's old sweet silvery tones returned, and with them his dreams, still alive, singing once more.

Meter Running

Hesitant first light. Dying leaves whispering on the condo lawn. Sodden air. Breeze bearing jet fuel, bacon. Stomach begging. Maddie zipped her windbreaker, crunched to her cab.

Her boyfriend Dan hadn't come home again. *Is three nights a pattern?* Not even Ohm to join her in sleeplessness. Poor mutt cooped up overnight at the clinic. *Bet he's confused. Probably dying. Why do all those tests? Because you have hope. Or try to have it.*

Maddie caressed the door handle. The door unlocked electronically. She liked testing this zippy little Prius, hoped the company would make the cars permanent. Not your usual taxi.

She hauled out a rag, wiped condensation from the windshield.

Something shifted. She looked up. The sunrise was cupped perfectly in a graceful dip in the dark foothills. A momentary crucible of light.

Maddie felt hopeful. And hungry. She hurried to finish wiping, stopped. There was the faint outline of a fingered heart high on the glass.

Her pulse jumped. *Dan? Shit, more likely a Prius admirer. Dan would have scribbled 'Wash me' or 'Lose some weight, Mad'.* She sighed. Nothing like a jerk for a boyfriend. *Where the hell is he?*

She snapped the rag at leaves littering the roof, jumped in, started the engine and rolled off. The Prius moved in silence. The leaves crinkled and groused.

As usual, Maddie's breakfast at the Capri—her only guaranteed meal on double shift days—included too many goodies. Why the cinnamon roll on top of everything else? But she savored the last plate-scrape of icing, accepted a coffee refill.

Time. She squeakslid across the orange vinyl booth, avoiding the ancient duct tape.

"Car Four rolling. Good morning!"

"'morning, Maddie." Even through the small speaker, Penny's voice was clover honey. Maddie thought the owner made a really smart move hiring his grandmother as a dispatcher. Penny could be a drill sergeant, but often she coddled her drivers. "OK, sweetheart. You can start off with Sally. She's at the Riverside."

Maddie turned up 27th. Immediately braked hard to avoid a meditating squirrel. She tried not to hit squirrels. She'd worked out their little patterns. Run into the road. Hesitate. Run forward or hip-hop back. Maddie kept track of casualties. This week alone: eight misses but three hits. Indecision kills. She was beginning to understand indecision.

Dan couldn't make up his mind. Not good for a lawyer. Not good for a boyfriend either. And now these absences. He said it was hunting season. Meantime, Maddie's own indecision held them in this stupid little dance, the death dance of another relationship. Shit, she hadn't gotten that fat, had she? Compensatory eating. Downsizing, career change, seriously-ill mother, dying dog. Didn't everyone have those things to deal with? *Oh, did I forget uncertain future?*

Sally Revere was a regular. A professional girl cum student. She flounced out of the Riverside, swung open the door and sat up front. Swishes of silk. Swirls of Evening in Paris, reminding Maddie of her grandmother's favorite perfume. *Jeez, they still make that stuff?*

Sally stretched and yawned. "I love it when I get to keep the room, my own bath and all. Hey, girl. How's it going?"

"So so, I guess." They swung out of the lot. "Might have to put my dog down."

"Shit, that's a bummer."

"Yep. I've had Ohm over ten years."

"Huh. Om? Like the chant?"

Maddie laughed. "Almost. I was an electrical engineer, and when my puppy showed resistance to training, I named—God, that shithead!"

She braked heavily to avoid a cyclist shooting across Chinden. The idiot disappeared up a side street. "Give me a squirrel any day."

"What?"

Maddie's next fare was another regular. Go had only one name. And only one eye. Once a week she drove Go from his trailer park to the VA. He was a walnut in jeans—short, squat, browned and extremely wrinkled. His good eye glared sideways. His mangled socket reached for the sky.

Go muttered a lot. Mostly to himself. Today he surprised her.

"Like your color, Missy."

"My color?"

"Your taxi, maxi. Red. I dig it. Red.

"Toyota calls it Barcelona Red. Ole! Bring on the bulls."

Her little joke didn't connect. He leaned toward her. "Blood ain't red, you know. Blood's anger. Anger and bile and piss. That ain't red."

She nodded.

"Ever killed anyone, Missy?"

"No, I would never..." Maddie could feel his twisted smile.

"Ain't no never, Nancy. See red, make dead. You wait."

Penny dispatched Maddie to the North End. The Prius scattered leaves in its wake, the bright red cleaving russets and golds.

The house was a classic 20's bungalow, a charmer. But its owner was a sourfaced senior. He came out lugging a grubby suitcase and a bad attitude.

"Airport." No "Good morning."

He frowned at the Prius, seemed surprised when his case fit in the trunk. Climbed into the back seat. Checked his watch. Stared inwardly. Maddie radioed Penny.

"Four to the port."

"All right, dear." Not conventional dispatcher-speak.

Meter Running

Maddie's imagination was embellishing stories about her passenger—she made him a mortician headed to a zombie convention—when her cell rang. Her spirits rose, anticipating Dan. It was the vet.

"Bad news, Madelyn." The vet's petside manners stank. "Serious liver troubles, abdominal pain, internal bleeding. I suggest we put him down."

"I was afraid of that..."

"'course, we could do surgery, try other meds, maybe keep him going a few more months. What do you think?"

They agreed she could mull it over and call him back.

"Sorry," she said in the mirror to the passenger. "Dying dog."

"Tough," he said, looking at his watch. "How much longer? I got a dying aunt and a sonofabitch bunch of greedy cousins waiting in Houston."

After Maddie dropped off the mortician—who surprised her by tipping generously—she radioed to ask if she could squeeze in a stop at the nursing home.

"Listen, sweetie," said Penny, "take all the time you need. You only got one mother."

But what a mother. Most of her life, Lorena Ivers had been distant and unloving. Most of her life she had treated Maddie at best dismissively, at times with cruel dispassion. Now she seemed to want to reconnect even as a trifecta of diseases and dementia ebbed her life. Desperation often flashed in her eyes.

Maddie was conflicted. Old resentments and disappointments stubbornly competed with duty, sympathy and a feeling which might have been love trying to bubble up. All set against the running down of the clock.

This was spiff-up-the-ladies day at Sagehaven. Lorena's thin hair was primped, blued and fluffed. Her pink fleece nightgown was as yet unsullied. They'd doused her in gingery cologne. It didn't mask other smells.

"Hi, Mom. How're you doing?" The daily greeting.

Lorena half-smiled, blinked, dropped into puzzlement. She turned and stared out the small window at a stunted maple. Her oxygen device sputtered.

This morning nothing Maddie said could get a response. She sat beside her mother, thinking about Dan, about Ohm. Three more leaves drifted away from the maple. Lorena's breath rasped, settled.

Maddie stared at Lorena. The familiar face, almost serene in its blankness, belied decades of sneers, cutting remarks and cynical observations. It belied Lorena's withholding of love, her denial of tenderness. All Maddie's adult life she had feared turning into her mother, fought against the sourness which had been constantly modeled for her. Even now, despite her mother's condition, on every visit to Sagehaven Maddie had to battle an upwelling bitterness. Lorena hadn't cared. Why should she?

Maddie stood, lightly kissed her mother's forehead. Past time to go.

Meter Running

She held her breath against the hallway odors. Chicken soup, furniture polish, finality. Outside, she gulped in the fresh damp air, feeling guilty. Yet again.

Life and color exploded into the cab. Nardelie Muamba wore a Congolese *pagne* and head wrap. A tumult of gorgeous fall prints with adventurous textures. A hubbub of musk and peppermint.
"*Hujambo*, Miss Maddie! *Bonjour*! Refugee office, please."
How to sound happy when you're in distress. Boise's refugees were a study in strength. Maddie knew some of Nardelie's family were trapped in the camps, others threatened by M23 rebels. But Nardelie had a bright, Grand Canyon smile.
"Today we try harder to get my cousin Lys out. They say her husband was killed."
"I'm so sorry."
"I fear for her."
"Your persistence will help. Oops! Do you understand 'persistence?'"
"*Oui!*" Nardelie laughed. "It's my middle name!"
"And funny too! I'm envious. How can you deal with—everything?"
"In my country, they say when you must go out on a thin tightrope between life and the other, you learn how to run."
"I wish you good luck, *bon chance*."
"*Wewe ni aina sana.* You are very kind, Miss Maddie."

Ohm was uppermost in Maddie's thoughts. She needed to call the vet. She needed to have it out with Dan. Some days required too many decisions.

She made another airport run then picked up food for a downtown office party.

"Our van fritzed out at the worst time," said the caterer. She handed Maddie a large bag. "For you. Chipotle specials. Enjoy."

After the delivery, Maddie sped along Bannock. Ran a yellow at 15th, breathed deeply. She pulled over, dodging a cyclist slaloming through a shower of golden leaves.

Lunch, maybe. She inspected a sandwich, picked stray cilantro from the artisanal bread, nibbled, quit, half-laughed. "Well, I can stand to lose a pound or three... Or so I'm told." She picked up her cell to call Dan, but found herself dialing the vet's. No change, except maybe slightly for the worse.

Some things were inevitable. *Poor Ohm.* The vet wanted a decision.

"OK, I guess we'll do it," Maddie whispered. "But I want to be there. I could manage this afternoon. What time will work?"

She texted Dan about Ohm. *3:30. Come if u can.*

Work was a way to stave off sorrow. Well, to postpone it. Maddie checked back in and was glad to drive up on the Bench to fetch another regular.

Mrs. Pumphrey was a walking tobacco factory. The cab needed airing whenever she'd sat in it. But she amused Maddie during their nicotine runs. The assisted

Meter Running

living facility had a perfectly good senior van, but Mrs. P. wanted to zip around on her own schedule, varying where she went for her fix.

"Move about, more exercise...for my mind," she'd laugh, with a high wheeze descant.

Mrs. Pumphrey was waiting in the driveway. Her tiny head peeked out from an outrageous and outdated green and black checkered coat.

"Hey, Maddie, whadya say?" She coughed. "Let's hit Hannifan's. I'm thinking a big cigar. I'll get you one too."

Maddie helped Mrs. P. into the passenger seat. "Hannifan's it is. But nothing for me, thanks."

"It's a phallic thing, you know. Cigars." Wheeze. "For men. The ones who need to compensate." Chuckle. "Lots of those!" Wheeze. "But me? I just like the taste."

Mrs. P. prattled on. Maddie allowed herself as much distraction as she could. Ohm's life was on an ever-shortening leash. Dan had not returned her text. Her stomach protested.

Their foray into town netted Mrs. P. a cigar in a red velveteen case and two soft packs of Turkish cigarettes.

"These little buggers are killers. But I love 'em!"

Back at Treasure Gardens, Mrs. Pumphrey clambered out. Leaned on the Prius. Hawked a glob of brown phlegm onto the sidewalk.

"They said I'd be dead eleven years ago. What did they know? See ya, Maddie."

Maddie's next call was only five minutes away. She'd picked up Esmee Black several times. Esmee's small gray bungalow was hidden among a stand of tall cottonwoods. Maddie thought the gaunt trees threatened to topple any day. Esmee said she'd take her chances.

"Ain't gonna cut down no trees," she announced. "Life's too precious."

All of Esmee's trips involved St. Luke's. Esmee was dealing with cancer. She was upfront about it. Yet another round of treatments. The struggle continues.

They headed off. Esmee adjusted her headscarf, a vivid and defiant blue.

"Chemo again," she sighed. "Them nurses are sweet, but some of 'em seems worn down. Hard not to, I guess, all that dying they sees."

Maddie turned down Americana. "How are you holding up, Miz Esmee?"

"Oh, OK, I guess. You gotta try." Esmee's eyes widened. "Hey, watch that squirrel! Dumb little critters, ain't they? But yeh, you gotta try."

Maddie veered into the bike lane, already second-guessing the squirrel. *Nine misses. Another chance to play God.*

The wall clock in the vet's lobby was a fat ceramic spaniel. Blotchy black spots. Big eyes rolling. Pendulum tail wagging. Tick, tick. Maddie once thought it cute. Not today.

3:29 and no Dan. Arf, arf.

The receptionist, murmuring with professional sympathy, led Maddie to an examining room. Ohm dozed on a mat. He opened his eyes, struggled to stand. Maddie hugged him. He seemed almost his usual affectionate slobbery self. But not quite. She wondered if he knew something was up.

The vet came in, explained the sequence, injected Ohm with a sedative, left the room.

Maddie sat with her increasingly woozy dog. He flopped back on the mat. She stroked his back. The room smelled of damp fur and rubbing alcohol.

She tried to slow time down. Tried to will the vet to be urgently needed elsewhere. Thought about Lorena. Ohm shuddered and passed gas.

The door opened. The vet muttered something, lifted Ohm up onto the table, shaved a paw, stuck in a needle. Pressed the plunger.

Maddie was back in the cab before she knew it. She sat there, holding Ohm's clunky old collar, twisting it like a rosary.

That's what death is, she thought—*a blur of busyness: sedative, shave, lethal shot, eyelids flutter, breathing stops, last hug, commiserations, paperwork, 'cash or credit?'*

A covey of sycamore leaves darted about in the wind. *Done.*

Maddie clicked Ohm's leash and his collar together and coiled them beside her seat. *Nothing left but tears and a lifetime void.*

It was good to resume the routine. Penny, extra kindness in her voice, dispatched her here and there.

Pick up and deliver Mr. Lamolinara's laundry. As usual, he was too busy to fetch it himself. *How can a taxidermist have so much work?*

Take a car buyer to the cluster of dealers on Fairview. "Old Chevy finally up and died on me," he said, boring Maddie with anecdotes about cars he'd cherished.

Back to St. Luke's for another chemo patient. Petite Mrs. Fremont, a regular, nervously adjusted her oversized wig the entire way to her apartment, never getting it quite right. Usually she was very talkative, but today she didn't say much. She flexed her dental plates over and over. It looked like she was practicing her smiling.

Night was arriving quickly. Far off, the western end of the valley was still aflame under orange clouds, but in town the light was wan, the trees shivered, the fallen leaves hunkered in darkening piles.

Maddie made a quick run home. The condo was dark and chilly. No sign of Dan. She ate leftover pasta, not bothering to heat it, grimaced at some sour milk, remembered a box of Girl Scout cookies, crunched on them as she returned to the cab. Mint and chocolate. Life still had something to offer.

Penny had gone home. The evening dispatcher was Karl Sites, a letch. She hated the way his voice drooled, salivated over the airwaves. His tongue seemed to curl out of the radio. She cringed, wanted to wash her ears.

"Tally ho, Car Four! Maddie, how are you, luv?" Karl affected an English accent. He was from Denton, Texas. "To the aerodrome, would you? Schusters, party of two. Toodling along to Eagle, pet."

Meter Running

Her fares stood at the Will Call curb, knee-deep in baggage. As Maddie rolled up, Mrs. Schuster glowered, pulling her coat to her neck. Her husband flourished his watch. Their luggage and Mrs. Schuster's overbearing perfume filled every cranny of the Prius. It would be a long run to Eagle.

The Schusters didn't stop sniping at each other. Maddie, thoughts elsewhere, heard snippets of 'you should have', 'why didn't you?', 'he was your goddam uncle,' 'funerals suck', 'well, don't blame me,' 'whose fault is that?'.

When 'should have' spat out for the fourth time or fifth time, Maddie made a note to try to be more giving—and forgiving—the next time she an Dan had an argument. *If there still is a we.* She turned on the headlights.

She glanced in the mirror and saw Mr. Schuster scowling.

"They should put old folk out to pasture and throw away the key." For punctuation he pulled down his Broncos cap.

They were stingy tippers. Maddie was happy to drop them off and head back towards Boise. She powered down her windows to clear the air.

"**B**ig night ahead,' said Sally Revere. "Hope so anyway." Sally looked stunning in black velvet, long silver chains and huge dangling hoop earrings.

Maddie signaled a turn. "How's school going?"

29

"Don't ask. Shit, I'm supposed to be studying for something better, but who knows? I think I want to move out of the game. But the money's good."

Maddie pulled into the Ameritel parking lot. The hotel's neon lights sputtered on. Sally pulled out a voucher.

"Dead end life, eh?"

"One of these days maybe Mr. Right will show up."

Sally opened the door. "That'd be John Right, right?"

They laughed.

"OK, luv. Off you go to Penguilly's." Maddie felt Karl leering into the microphone. "A Mr. Vernon's waiting outside. He's in a cammo jacket, dearie."

Maddie drove downtown to the bar strip, double-parked by Penguilly's. A tall, skinny man in his early 30's stepped off the curb, opened the passenger door and slid in.

"Mr. Vernon?"

"Yeah, well. It's Quentin. Don't matter." Nervous and high. He reeked. Cigarettes, beer, sweat. Something rancid.

"Where are we going?"

He gave her an address in Indian Lakes. She radioed it to Karl as she pulled into traffic.

Maddie felt the guy watching her. He talked with a quick staccato. "Quentin. You know. Like the director? Quentin Tarantula. That guy. Great movies."

As they turned right on Fourth, she glanced at him. Seemed to have the jitters. Twitched. *Like a squirrel. Sheesh, a big squirrel in my cab.*

"Taran... I don't think I know his films," she ventured, slowing for two erratic jaywalkers.

She felt his double take. "Not 'Pulp Fiction?' 'Kill Bill'? I mean. Fucking filmmaker's movies."

"Sorry, no. You make films?"

He drew out a laugh. It reminded her of the screech of the gate at Lorena's nursing home.

"Maybe. Sorta. In my head, I guess. Movies. I sorta plot things out."

"Sounds like a real talent."

He snorted. "Yeah, sure. Lotta good it does me." Another snort. *If he spits, I'll shove him out the door.*

They headed along Front toward the connector freeway. Maddie wanted to get rid of this guy. *Sooner the better.* She also wanted to finish her shift. Track down Dan. Go home and cry. *Poor Ohm.*

He cleared his throat. "You ever want it? Be in a movie?"

"Me? God, no."

"You got the looks."

"Thank you. But I'm not the movie type."

"Could be a star."

They passed under a streetlight, and she saw his teeth exposed and gleaming. *Ready for an acorn.*

He nodded. "I could do it."

"Excuse me?"

"Make you a star, Maddie." Nod, nod.

Something bothered her. After a moment, it hit her. "How do you know my name?"

His laugh was as phony as Karl's accent. "Doesn't everyone? Know you? Maddie?"

Of course! He saw it on the registration card. She was chastising her suspicious mind when Quentin piped up again.

"I asked. For you. Specially."

"Why would you do that?"

"Don't you know me?"

"I'm sorry, but..."

"Condo around back. From yours. Neighbors. You and me."

The speed limit was 60. Maddie pushed it to 65. *Get rid of this guy.*

His voice became shy. No staccato. "I left you a message, Maddie."

"I'm sorry? A message?" Suddenly she realized what he meant. *The heart on the windshield. Not Dan. Shit. This creep.*

"Oh, yes, very sweet. Thank you." But not appropriate, Mr. Quentin. I don't know you." She edged their speed up to 70. "Anyway, I have a boyfriend."

That snicker again. "Boyfriend? I seen him—that guy—moving out."

"Moving...? No, he just went hunting."

"Hunting, huh? I seen him with other babes. Down the courthouse. Yeah. He hunts babes. Not as hot as you."

Maddie took the Cole exit, stopped at a signal.

"Look, Quentin or Vernon or whoever you are. I'm letting you off at the mall."

"No. Turn left. South. That's the plan." He rustled inside his jacket. "This here makes it so."

Meter Running

The gun was ugly. A phallus. Maddie's heart lurched.

"And don't touch the radio." Her hand jerked back.

Humor. I need humor.

She forced a laugh. "I get it! We're trying out one of your movies, right?"

"Oh, yeah. It's my movie! Got it scripted. In my head." The light changed. "Turn. Left."

Reluctantly she turned. Her mind raced ahead. *What's along this way? Commercial, commercial, subdivisions, subdivisions, a few farms, desert. Desert?*

"Why don't we do a scene at the cineplex?" she said. "I'll turn in there."

"No you won't."

"Could be fun—do your film around all those movies theaters?"

"Not in the script, Maddie. You know that."

"What do you want?

He didn't answer.

They drove up the hill, past the bright Mormon temple, past the turn to the cineplex. Further and further south. Less and less light. Fewer and fewer people.

"I've watched you. Maddie." he said. "You're too good. For that guy."

"What do you want?"

"Life's not fair. But you can grab. What you deserve. That's in the films. Tarantula's."

Two dark shapes vaulted into the road. Deer. They stiffened in the headlights. Maddie braked hard and swerved. Something clinked. Quentin slammed into his door. But he swung the gun back even as Maddie began to reach for her own door.

"Don't do it. This ain't no prop."

The white tails vanished into dark shrubbery.

"It's killed people. Af-fucking-ghanistan."

"Look, if you need help..."

"Shut up and drive." He chuckled. "That line? 'Shut up and drive?' In 32 movies. At least. I counted. But I mean it. Drive."

She held the speed down as much as she dared. They rolled south. Lights became rarer. The desert darkness stretched before them. Quentin trembled, twitched. He seemed to be rubbing his abdomen. But he kept the gun up. Maddie tried to slow her breathing. Tried to think of options.

In any other cab she'd have had a panic button. But not the Prius, still only a test unit. No driver alarm, no emergency GPS, no one-way listening from the office. She was on her own.

Quentin exhaled. He told Maddie to slow down. Directed her into a small dirt lane. It wandered and twisted through grass and bumps, between stunted trees. No lights. No houses.

"Stop!" Now he was breathing hard. Maddie stopped the cab.

"Turn off the engine. Now!" She pressed the off button but left the headlights on.

"Look, you don't want to—"

"Don't. Don't tell me. What I want. Got it figured." He shuddered. "OK. There's a shack. Down there." He gestured with the gun. "Let's go."

Meter Running

Maddie froze. Her right hand touched something bulky beside her hip. *Ohm's leash and collar.* She clenched it. *Anything.*

"Out, Maddie! You and me. Out!"

She half-turned, pulled the coiled leash into her lap, and opened the door. Quentin was already bounding out his side. He was quick. But the car was between them. As he moved to the front, she slid towards the rear.

"Cute, Maddie! Uh-uh! Fun's this way."

He was in the headlights, squinting. A deer.

No, a squirrel.

Maddie had learned how to second-guess squirrels. Instead of retreating, she stepped away from the car. Quentin rounded the front. Came toward her.

She feinted left. Reached her arm back.

He froze. Thought. Lunged right. Directly into the swinging arc of the leash and the heavy collar. The tangle jangle of dog tags and buckles caught him across the nose. He screamed. Maddie stepped in and kicked him in the crotch. Viciously. He collapsed, moaning.

Thank you, Ohm.

She picked up the gun, locked herself in the cab, got on the radio. For once Karl wasn't smarmy. He assured her the cops wouldn't be long. And no English accent.

Outside, a dark lump, Quentin remained curled on the ground. Maddie could hear an occasional whimper.

This is raptor territory, she thought. *Maybe something grand, fierce, and hungry will dive and put him out of his misery.*

On her way home, nerves still unsettled, Maddie had the impulse to detour to Sagehaven.

Tonight the tang of sage graced the nursing home entrance. For once, in the hallway lavender trumped urine.

Lorena, wrapped in a crazy quilt, was slumped in her easy chair, slowly wheezing oxygen, staring out the window at the darkness. She blinked but didn't move when Maddie touched her shoulder.

"Came by to say I love you, Mom. That's all. I love you."

Nothing. Maddie sighed. She gave Lorena a half-hug, stood there a long moment, went to the door.

"Eat your cupcake, Madelyn." The voice was low and feathery. Maddie looked back. Lorena had partly-turned. A feeble smile pushed through the confusion.

"I will, Mom, I will. I'll have my cupcake and eat it too."

Her mother blinked again and slowly faced away, already retreating from a last ember's flaring.

Maddie drove home. Her condo windows were dark. She sat in the Prius. Checked her cell phone. No voice mail. No texts.

Rain spattered the windshield. She watched the drops push at a lone maple leaf, resisted crying. Out beyond the blurred clouds she saw fragments of clearing night sky and the bright edge of the rising moon.

"Well, guess what, Quentin," she said aloud. "I'm about to rewrite my own script."

Room Enough

Crickets sang to a cloudless night. Garth, smoking, perched on a stubborn stump near the edge of his pasture and stared up at the Milky Way. Except for a guardian battalion of sharp white starpoints, it was blurred, ambiguous. A shroud, he thought, a coffin liner, its soft, infinite folds ready for unambiguous death.

He exhaled slowly, pensively. The smoke curled close, reluctant to drift into the dark. A frog queried the shadows.

Garth smelled of tobacco, maple syrup and musky cologne. At supper, he'd indulged in creamy pancakes, swirling them with slow, golden sweetness, and the syrup still teased his tongue. The cologne was a habit. Or maybe clinging to something. It made him laugh, if harshly, when he thought about it. His wife said the scent turned her on. The same wife who, one dazzling winter morning, took off with their minister, leaving the small town in great confusion.

A shocked flock, Garth liked to joke to ease his pain. God had run off too, he thought. God no longer hung around here. Life kept proving that. As to the cologne, well, some remained in the bottle, so Garth still slapped it on, defiant. Maybe the wind would sweep the fragrance all the way across Idaho to Wyoming or Montana, where Sara would sniff, wrinkle her nose, remember, yearn, return.

Once more the frog heralded desire, startling the crickets into a brief silence. Carefully, Garth tamped the remains of his cigarette against his boot and fieldstripped the butt. For a final moment, he stared at the stars, then he turned and trudged towards the work shed, where his current project awaited.

He'd been making coffins for many years. Kinda funny, he'd say to anyone who inquired, but the whole deal came from my teenage stint as a supermarket stock boy. I often had to break up wooden crates and pallets, and for some reason I started reshaping them into coffins. Dunno why exactly. The things just fascinated me. Maybe I was already thinking about mortality. It seems I was a natural, so I apprenticed to Old Man Sloane. I became darn good at it. Much better than him, better even than folk in the bigger towns.

Garth's parents had visions of his becoming a doctor. They wanted to get him off the ranch, away from hardscrabble, into whitecollar. But the shingle he hung out was Garth McCready, Coffin Maker. Master builder of small, thoughtful rooms for the last great transition.

In time, Garth became a specialist in unique, artistic coffins, crafted with fine woods, distinctive fittings and embellishments, enhanced with unusual engravings, each built with an unerringly singular eye.

There was one irony. Garth discovered he had a phobia. Whenever he drew close to finishing a coffin, he had to fight harder and harder not to imagine himself inside, trapped in suffocating eternity. Shuddering, he would rush outdoors to take breaks, gasping, blinking for light, breathing in the whole wide Idaho sky, before forcing himself back to the task.

Tonight, Garth switched on the bright workshed spotlights. Cradled on a padded gurney was an elegant mahogany coffin, almost finished. It was perfectly milled, painstakingly edge-glued, meticulously grain-aligned. Beautifully incised on the long perimeter was a motif of tiny animals and birds—rabbits, deer, wolves, foxes, eagles, hawks, and here and there, lovingly incongruous, some teddy bears.

The coffin was full-sized, not for a child. But in it soon would lie the once-child of his dreams, Garth's only son Trevor, grown to manhood in this desert, slain in another desert far across the world. For what purpose Garth had no idea. Freedom, democracy, greed, stupidity, insanity. He supposed war was all of those things. For sure it was always false glory, real loss.

Garth breathed in deeply. He loved the smell of fine woods, lacquers, oils. At this moment, linseed held the high notes, riding on the somber baritones of curing oak. Slowly shaking a tin of varnish, he moved around the coffin, inspecting.

The two immaculate military officers who had driven in to see him, trailing dust, nudging tumbleweeds, had shown no surprise when this tall, rangy, sad-eyed man, hearing their news, had sagged just a little, quickly straightened, and responded, "Then I'll make his coffin."

Garth put down the tin. He caressed the smooth, gleaming sides of the coffin, ran his fingers lightly over the line of animals, remembered Trevor in his dress uniform, so smart, so slim, so young, so full of—what? Promise? Optimism? Idealism?

Garth knew those things well from his own youth. They'd been honed, whittled, chiseled, turned on the lathe of years, fashioned into some form of acceptance. You watched the family acreage slowly diminish. You woke up to learn your wife had run off with the preacher. You made coffins, knowing what each signified, no matter how great your artistry. And now you were building a coffin for your son. What does all that amount to? What size does a box have to be to contain a life? How big does a heart need to be to hold all its grief?

In the barn next door, a goat bleated vigorously. Two sheep fussed back. The wisdom of ruminants, Garth thought, smiling faintly.

On impulse, he unlocked the gurney wheels and rolled the coffin outside. In the center of the yard, he reset the wheels, paused and took a long, slow breath. He shucked off his boots, hesitated again, then climbed up into the coffin, lay back and looked up.

Claustrophobia squeezed, pressed, threatened, but the sight of the stars released him, kept him unrestrained.

A slight breeze wrapped him in the poignancy of woodsmoke. Crickets and frogs chirred and croaked in selfish syncopation.

Garth cushioned his hands under his head, sighed, and gazed steadily skyward.

Room Enough

Unnoticed, a small curl of wood nestled beside him in the coffin. Into this stowaway slid one lone, heavy teardrop, glistening and mute.

Under the Hood

What was in the baby carriage?

The entire neighborhood was dying to know. Stock markets never experienced such speculation.

Every evening, curtains slid aside, doors cracked open, shrubs parted, leashed dogs panted in place as owners sneaked chance glances. But there were no revelations.

What on earth was in that baby carriage?

This was none of your ordinary modern strollers or flashy transformer baby buggies. It was one of those big old-fashioned perambulators. Large wheels, each with an intricate web of spokes. Oversized springs, poised and tense. Deep bassinette shrouded with a dark double canopy which could hide anyone. Or anything.

This baby carriage was Victorian, funereal. Absorbent black suggested utter seriousness. Slivers of keen chrome kept an eye out for anyone approaching too close.

Every evening at 6:03, Mr. Kohl pushed the pram down the cracked walkway of his blank-faced bungalow. Never earlier, never later.

Bill Francis, directly opposite, got in the habit of checking his watch. Annie Burke, next door to Bill, skipped the opening of her beloved "Jeopardy" to stare and wonder. "Baby carriages for 1,000, Alex."

Mr. Kohl, small but not dapper, virtually featureless, drawn into himself, looking at no one, saying nothing, in a dark suit, dark tie, black teardrop-crown Fedora, black leather gloves, rolled the carriage to the sidewalk, turned right, and pushed west. If it was chilly, add a black woolen topcoat. If it was raining, add a black umbrella.

 Each night Mr. Kohl and the carriage returned from the east at exactly 7:04. Disappeared along the side walkway of his house.

 The Thompsons, neighbors on that side, bemoaned their blank garage wall. They lusted for an auspicious observation post. Agonized over adding a window. Thrashed things out. Measured, estimated. Bickered, left the wall blank. Simmered in impotence, yearned for x-ray vision.

If Mr. Kohl intrigued the neighborhood, it was his perambulator which enflamed everyone's curiosity.

 "It's like a huge raven, brooding," said Mrs. Gerwig, addicted to simile.

 Miss Roseforth nibbled homemade shortbread. "It reminds me of a coffin on wheels." Her breath was butter and allspice.

 "A coffin? Yes. And that odd little man..." Mrs. Gerwig raised her demitasse. "...is very much like an undertaker."

 Morning teas and afternoon coffee klatches had a new focus. Something delicious on which to munch.

 What was in that baby carriage? What was underneath that black hood?

 Nary a clue. Nary a diaper trail.

Under the Hood

And then there was Mr. Kohl himself. Mystery neighbor. Enigmatic pram- pusher. The type, everyone thought, who'd scare away the welcome wagon.

In the days after he moved in, there was never an answer to the doorbell or to friendly knockknuckles. The neighbors, obligatory fresh-baked treats in hand, soon stopped visiting his tiny thin-stooped porch. They felt slightly stupid standing there. They empathized with travelling salesmen.

After poor Mrs. Carmichael's death, the bungalow had sat empty for months. Not even a For Sale sign. Nothing to suggest the hope of rebirth. Then one evening, out walked a small man pushing a big black baby carriage. The pattern began. Someone was again living there. No one remembered seeing a moving van.

They knew nothing about Mr. Kohl aside from his surname, and that was learned only by accident. A single piece of mail was misdelivered to 309 instead of to 306. Sally Lawson took proper note—and made notes—before walking over with the errant letter. She pushed the envelope through the heavy-lipped black metal letter-slot, the sole accoutrement on a dark and uninviting door.

Sally reported—to any who might be interested, and there were plenty of those—that her lucky find bore nothing but the printed words, MR. KOHL, the address and a cancelled stamp, no return information. To her not-infrequent regret, Sally had stopped short of steaming open the envelope.

Mr. Kohl never was spied out in his small yard. Soon after his arrival, two gloomy workmen scuttled about for a few hours. Since then, the yard sat dark-barked and black-mulched corner to corner, daring plants to intrude. Even weeds stayed away.

Weekdays, weekends, no one ever saw Mr. Kohl except on his pram perambulations.

"Guess he's not an 8 to 5 man." said Ruth Kinnear to her live-in mother, Peg. "No! Correction! He's a 6:03 to 7:04 man." She snickered. "Maybe he's going to a part-time job."

Peg raised an eyebrow. "Can't imagine what'd that'd be. Unless he works in a baby buggy factory." She laughed herself into an attack of hiccups.

Comics abounded in this neighborhood.

No neighbor, whether sharp of hearing or by coincidence trying out an Army/Navy parabolic microphone, ever heard a sound coming from Mr. Kohl's house. Not a baby's cry, not a chortle, not a whimper, not a lullaby. Nor a bit of jazz, nary a fragment of Beethoven, a doowop of bop, a silly syllable of rap. No singing in the shower. No shower.

At number 306, silence ruled.

No neighbor, whether casually curious or exceptionally-vigilant, ever saw visitors at Mr. Kohl's house. Once in a rare while Larry the Mailman put an envelope through the slot.

When pressed about number 306—which was often—Larry was mum.

"Privacy trumps all." Larry reeked of mothballs. "US Postal Code, Section 75-Q. Ask me about bowling, my

Under the Hood

tole painting, my cocker spaniel. Anything. Except don't ask about someone else's mail."

"10-4," said Chet Simpson. "Zip codes mean zipped mouths." He zipped his lips.

Krista Tyler persisted. Had Larry ever peeked through the slot? Ever seen a baby carriage? The mailman was horrified.

"Voyeurism is cause for dismissal. Postal Code 1259-B."

What's in that baby carriage? The neighborhood now had a mantra.

"Let's start a pool," suggested Johnny McLeod. "List all possibilities, ante up, make our picks, winner takes all." He dabbed his shiny pate, proud beacon of the neighborhood.

His wife shook her head. "How's that going to work? How'll we ever know what's in there?" Bernice rechecked her cards. "Two clubs."

"Pass." Nan Simpson stretched for the bridge mix. "Of course we could mug him." She tossed chocolate raisins toward her mouth. One escaped, somersaulted onto the table.

"Mug him? Mug the buggy?" Chet Simpson crunched a cashew. "How about we club the buggy? Hug the mugger? Mug the—"

"Chet..."

"OK. I bid five mugs. Sorry, I mean five clubs."

What was in that blanket-blank baby carriage?

47

Talk was becoming cheap and the gossip cheep-cheep-cheep, so some of the curious made attempts to follow Mr. Kohl on his carriage-pushing rounds.

Sam and Gloria Mitchell, titillated to be sleuthing, took their poodle Sun King out for a long stroll, perfectly timed so they could hang back a half-block from Mr. Kohl.

All went well until Sun King stopped to wet an oft-saluted fencepost. Up ahead, Mr. Kohl and buggy turned the corner. When the Mitchells got there, dragging Sun King, the mystery man and pram had vanished. The bewildered poodle took the brunt of their lively invective.

Herb Clerwood decided to do some surreptitious shadowing in his wife Gail's oh-so-unobtrusive Smart Car. "Practically invisible," Herb announced, wresting the keys from Gail. She had her doubts. About the endeavor and about Herb's driving her new toy.

Herb let Mr. Kohl get a decent head start, then inched the small car along. Once again, a corner did in the enterprise. Pivoting the pram on its rear wheels, Mr. Kohl made a sharp right. Herb sped up. He reached the corner, drove onto the curb and clipped a fire hydrant.

The long yellow scratches were not a color match for Gail's (formerly) unblemished Smart Car. Over all, not a smart move.

Street corners seemed to be an issue, so Krista Tyler encouraged her latest gentleman friend to trot out at 5:55 p.m. and loiter well down the far side of the offending cross street. Krista promised Rupert a considerable amount of bliss should he come back with a good bit of reportage.

"If you see him as much as lean down to talk to that buggy, be sure to tell me. Bonus brownie points if you spot him open the thing." Wink. "Grand prize for reporting what's underneath the hood." Wink wink.

Rupert duly trotted out, debating whether he could get away with some heritage fibbing. Who'd know? Around the corner, on station, he continued his mulling. "Let's see, would they believe me if I saw a cat in there, maybe two? How about a stack of library books? That'd be neat."

Rupert's imagination was inversely proportional to his libido. While the young man was thus inventively engaged, Mr. Kohl pushed the pram right past the corner, not turning as before. Rupert missed him entirely. Krista was not moved to provide rewards.

What was in the baby carriage?

The Simpsons bribed their eight year old son to help solve the question. Chip could follow Mr. Kohl by pushing along behind him on a kick scooter. What could be more normal than a boy noodling up and down on an old-fashioned scooter? Nothing to arouse suspicion. Practically 19th Century. Normally Chip was a noisy young chap—he particularly liked drumming on garbage cans or clattering sticks on picket fences—but he was intrigued with the idea of stealth scootering.

Additionally, the bribe strongly appealed. In exchange for solid intel, his parents promised an upgrade for his hand-held gizmo. Chip had been hooked on electronics since age four. It was an easy sell.

Chip dusted off his scooter, in deep storage since little Alby Funston, all of seven, had razzed Chip about not riding something more cool. A little light oil, and snoop and scooter were ready to roll.

By 6 p.m. Chip was already bored with practice runs in front of his house. But at 6:03 his adrenalin awoke. A few doors away his prey emerged on the sidewalk. When Mr. Kohl rolled the black pram past Chip's driveway, the cunning lad was bending to tie a shoelace. He'd seen his share of spy movies. A few moments later, he revved up his pushing foot and scootered off in pursuit.

His parents and many neighbors were watching through narrow slits in their much-grasped curtains.

Chip kicked the scooter along with studied nonchalance, envisioning a cool undercover career in the FBI. He kept about fifty feet behind his assigned target.

At the second cross street, Mr. Kohl turned right. Just in case, Chip hot-footed it for a moment. His scooter made a pleasant clackety-clack on the pavement.

As he turned the corner, his cell phone rang. 'Rang' is a relative term, as he'd programmed the phone with a troop of shrieking monkeys. This produced a triple anxiety. First, the shrieks might alert his quarry. Second, Chip had been taught on penalty of electronic gadget suspension never to use his phone while in motion. And third, he saw that Mr. Kohl, who'd somehow gained considerable distance, was already turning another corner.

Conflicted, Chip stopped. He answered. Incredibly, it was his mother, whispering for no reason he could figure, "What's he doing? What's happening, Chipster?"

Under the Hood

"Jeez, Mom, nothing yet. But I'm losing him. Gotta go."

He cut Nan off mid-sentence. Muttering "Bad move, Mom," he fired up his footwork and zoomed to the next corner at Guinness Book speed.

Mr. Kohl and the baby carriage had disappeared. Shoot! No 5G upgrade. Moms could be so dumb.

What was in that baby buggy anyway?

Sugar Jenkins hit on what they all thought the perfect idea. "Let's fight fire with fire!"

"What, burn his house down?" asked Bill Francis. He wasn't the least alarmed. He'd have a fine view from his living room. He enjoyed a whiff of Sugar's Coco Noir.

"No, no," Sugar said sweetly. "I have a much more elegant plan."

She suggested putting someone with another baby carriage onto the evening streets. This ersatz parent would come alongside Mr. Kohl. "Baby ahoy!" They would engage in the inevitable tete-a-tete, pram-a-pram conversation. Surely carriage-pusher bonding was universal? Couldn't fail.

The neighbors loved it.

Everyone thought Sugar herself was the logical choice for pusher. Young enough to have a believable babe-in-buggy. Attractive enough to earn a second look. Charming enough to hold even a curmudgeon in her sway.

Sugar accepted the mission. A round of applause. Bill Francis inhaled more Chanel.

Two main problems yet to solve: a. Carriage. b. Baby.

They dug out an ancient perambulator from the many treasures in Sally Lawson's attic. "Mine, actually," Sally blushed. "I can't bear to give anything away." The canopy was trimmed with faded pink roses.

Johnny McLeod admired his image in a vintage pier glass. "Won't the, eh, period qualities arouse Mr. Kohl's suspicions?"

"He's a man," said Bernice McLeod. "Men haven't a clue about such things. You certainly never did. Do."

"Besides, his own baby carriage is old as sin," said Gloria Mitchell. "Why would he think this antique unusual?" Gloria heard a discreet ahem. "Oh, I mean—it's really beautiful, Sally. I love these roses."

Sally's pram became the baby carriage of choice.

Next, the maybe-baby debate: real infant or doll?

"Does he really have to see what's in our buggy?" said Ken Toussant. "Is he that likely to look?"

"Well, he's not Mr. Sociable," Pete Zercher sucked on his pipe. "But this could break the ice. Melt his black heart. Make him want to reach out. Touch his Inner Daddy."

"I think you're going a bit far..."

"On the other hand," grumped Ruth Kinnear, "why not just swaddle up a stack of blankets and be done with it?" Lately she'd been thinking of stopping Mr. Kohl at gunpoint.

Annie Burke sipped her Darjeeling. "Oh no, at least a doll. For the shape, the heft."

"I'd opt for real," said Mrs. Gerwig, "Otherwise it would be like substituting cheddar for camembert, or, say, like using concrete instead of...Pavarotti."

This gave them pause.

In the end they voted for a live baby, cherub-cheeked, wafting talcum powder, cooing and fussing, fully-visible for the verisimilitude required of proper double dealing.

The Zerchers said they had a niece with a borrowable six-month old. Brittany was a baby of sturdy disposition and undoubtedly ready for her acting debut.

"Plus she already has undercover experience," said Chet Simpson. Only Peg Wilmot laughed. Or perhaps it was a half-suppressed hiccup.

Soon Sugar, made motherly, plus Sally's carriage, dusted and polished, plus Baby Brittany, newly fed, freshly-diapered, prepared to invade Mr. Kohl's secret world.

As a clever countermeasure to all the corner disappearances, Mommy Sugar was to roll Brittany off to the east at approximately 7:03 p.m., encountering Mr. Mystery Pram as he returned home. No corners remained. No escape possible. Maximum viewing for the window crowd. Video cameras optional.

And so it began. Sugar paraded on the sidewalk a few doors to the west of number 306. As her synchronized watch beeped 7:03, she slowly began to push her antique carriage east. In moments, as always, here came Mr. Kohl, almost as though appearing out of nowhere. The large black perambulator led the way, the chrome glinting thoughtfully. Sugar planned to screech to a halt in a police-style swerve to block the other carriage. Her heart did somersaults.

Mr. Kohl, resolutely pramming home, didn't appear to see them. His head was averted, his black Fedora, a jaunty hat on others, slumped like a dead crow on his head.

Countdown to the baby conference, to the grand uncovering. Ten, nine, eight...

Stage fright hits even the very young. Seven, six....Baby Brittany began wailing with an Ethel Merman set of lungs. Five, four...She bounced, shook. Three...Rocked and rolled. Two, one... Screamed.

They were almost prow to prow. Mr. Kohl ducked his head. Executed an impossible pirouette. Wrapped himself and his pram around Sugar and her baby. Twirled past them. Rolled up his walkway. All without making a sound.

Sugar was left with her mouth open. Brittany had her mouth open too, but she was far from speechless. Her wailing took on siren proportions. The onlookers didn't know what they'd seen. And each still had the same question.

What's in that damn pram?

Every effort they made to follow, intercept or second-guess, every effort failed. Mr. Kohl forever eluded them, never opened the canopy within anyone's view, often seemed to disappear en route.

People could only talk, fantasize, imagine.

Under the Hood

At the annual neighborhood picnic—to no one's surprise sans Mr. Kohl— everyone quickly jumped into the prime topic.

What's in it? There was a smorgasbord of conjectures.

Peg Wilmot burped. "Why not a cute little baby? Or even an ugly one?"

"Oh, baby, baby." Hal Brown mock-moaned at Krista Tyler, his new girlfriend.

Krista frowned at her barbecued shrimp.

Charlie Woost thought it most unlikely the carriage contained a real infant.

"Not a cry, not a squeal." Charlie was happy to be single and childless. "No baby's that quiet." Others murmured assent.

Charlie sighed. "Especially not in this neighborhood."

"If not a baby, then...?" Annie Burke probed her curried chicken. Too many grapes.

Barb Toussant, well-steeped in the teachings of Dr. Phil, proposed that the carriage might hold a favorite childhood toy—perhaps Mr. Kohl's teddy-weddy— something he'd never outgrown.

"Tell me you didn't just say 'teddy-weddy'," said Barb's husband, his mouth aglow with ketchup.

Barb ignored him. "Of course, he could be demonstrating an obsessional need for the baby he wants but for some reason can never have."

"I like that!" said Annie. "Could it be a trans-sexual obsession? His hat—it's creased just like a vagina, isn't it?"

All observed a moment of respectful visualization.

Cathy Niedermeyer theorized that Mr. Kohl could be trundling around his nanny's ashes. "Long ago she pushed him in that pram—now he's pushing her. Quite touching." Cathy smiled. "And very symmetrical."

Several liked the notion that the pram held an animal, maybe an unusual or illegal pet out for its nightly constitutional.

Herb and Gail Clerwood cheerfully pingponged with that idea. "Boa constrictor?" "Baby alligator?" "Pygmy grizzly?" "Twin chimps?"

"Smart Car?" stuck in Bill Francis. "That's a neat pet, eh Herb?" Herb quickly found something significant to study in the potato salad.

Harold Thompson put in a bid for a midget. Perhaps an elderly aunt, tiny and shy.

"Aunt Chloe is embarrassed to be seen, so he takes her out incognito."

"Is it politically correct"—Carrie Dixon crunched a potato chip—"to say 'midget'?"

Madge Thompson posited a murdered wife. Perhaps the lady's severed head was in the carriage? "He can't quite forgive himself for doing her in. He keeps rolling her about to show her the town."

"Heads will roll," Bill Francis grinned at Chet Simpson, whose mouth was stopped up with carrot-raisin salad.

Bob Robertson waved his mug. "It's pieces of her body. He distributes them bit by bit, night by night."

Under the Hood

Bob's beer sloshed and his wife cringed. "Forgive Bob's imagination," Penny said. "We just watched 'Rear Window'."

Johnny McLeod cleared his throat. "I don't want to scare anyone. But we could have a terrorist in our midst."

"Him? A terrorist?"

"Perfect cover. Maybe his baby buggy is carrying a bomb."

"But why the daily trips?"

"To get everyone used to it. Then—kaboom! Kablooey!"

"Slam, bam, thank you pram!" Chet Simpson mimed an explosion.

"Oh dear," said Miss Roseforth. "That wouldn't be good for the neighborhood." She was red-cheeked from sampling microbrews.

Hal Brown slurp-licked his popsicle. "It's his inflatable sex doll. Would fit in the buggy very nicely." Another lick. "They come in rubber or vinyl." More licks.

"How do you know about those?" Krista was seeing her latest squeeze in a new light.

The party continued, with the speculations generating much more interest than the twice-deviled eggs or the artificial rum balls.

In further scenarios, Mr. Kohl used the baby carriage to take away his empty whiskey bottles, tote trash to the dump, lug plastic to the recycling center, dispose of unspecified nasty items for The Mob.

"Since when is 'The Mob' around here?"

"Oh, they're everywhere. Just like aliens."

"That's it! Mr. Kohl's schlepping an alien! Didn't ET ride in a pram?"
"Em, I believe that was a bicycle basket."
Bernice McLeod clapped her hands. "It's his shopping cart! He makes nightly trips to Walmart. He's so embarrassed he hides everything in the baby buggy."
"We're all losing our marbles." Mrs. Gerwig folded her lawn chair. "We're like a gaggle of geese honking on and on. Honk, honk. Enough! We'll never have the answer until someone actually looks in that pram."
Mrs. Gerwig didn't know it, but her parting comments made someone's subconscious lick its lips. And not over the pickled artichokes.
What in hell is in that baby carriage? Said subconscious was going to find out. "Hey," it finally whooped, sending its owner a synaptic text, "Here's what you do, Nan!"

Nan Simpson was smarting from the barrage of comments from Chet and Chip about her careless phone call which ruined the scooter surveillance. She needed atonement. Payback. Something.
Nan skulked, observed. Nightly she was out on the street before 6:03, back again before 7:04. As cover, she walked Bluebell, her Welsh corgi. Bluebell was losing weight from all the extra exercise. Chet and Chip grumbled about tending to their own dinners.
Mr. Kohl continued his pram pushing, oblivious. Those rare times Nan and Bluebell were in his path, he shoved by effortlessly, the dog cower-diving to one side.

Under the Hood

Nan could never make eye contact. The man's acrid aftershave, if that's what it was, made her cringe.
    Soon Nan was a Nan with a plan.
    She decided that 7:04 was the best time. First, Mr. Kohl would be more tired then, thus less alert. Second, it was getting closer to dusk, reducing visibility. Third, the setting sun would be in his eyes.
    Thursday was the chosen night. At 6:03 Mr. Kohl wheeled his carriage away. Nan walked Bluebell until the dark figure disappeared. She took the dog home. Dressed in her jogging clothes. Gathered her supplies. Swigged a glass of merlot. Gathered her fortitude. If Chet and Chip sensed something was up, they didn't ask. In any case, they were too busy rummaging for dinner.
    A few minutes before seven, Nan approached number 306, lugging two heavy sacks. Bless Mrs. Gerwig for the idea! *We're losing our marbles.* Nan opened the sacks. She flooded the bottom of the driveway and much of the nearby sidewalk with little clear marbles. Hundreds. All came from the hardware store. None were pilfered from Chip's collection. No family blowback on this one.
    Nan tucked herself behind a tree in the front corner the yard at 308. Little danger of discovery. The Thompsons would be absorbed with television. They often bragged about viewing the "PBS News Hour". She suspected they were actually watching "Wheel of Fortune" just like the rest of the street. No matter.
    She peeked around the tree. Mr. Kohl was on time. Naturally. As he came closer to her glass army, she

realized there was a fortuitous extra: one wheel of the baby carriage was squeaking. Loudly. Like a very high, annoyed little voice. At first Nan thought it was a baby complaining. But it was a wheel. A spokes-person, she thought. *Oh God, you're as bad as Chet.*

Was Mr. Kohl distracted by the squeak? She thought so. She saw him lean slightly forward, jiggle the perambulator. But he kept moving. Toward her little landmines.

Nan backed away from the protection of the tree, looped up to the Thompson house, jogged casually back onto the sidewalk. Gauging her speed, she headed toward the marble zone.

Mr. Kohl, if he even saw her, was ignoring her. He bent toward the squeaking wheel. The carriage rolled into the marbles. Little clinkydinky noises. But no buggy deflection. Mr. Kohl, however, now marbleized, slip-skidded, tilted further forward, tried to stabilize by tightening his grip on the pram handle.

That's when jogger Nan hip-checked into the front end of the carriage. But her own feet went out from under her. *Oh-oh—not in the plan!*

She'd intended to necessitate a carriage stop, then to adlib—perhaps something clever like 'stand and deliver'.

But the laws of physics are mischievous. The combination of flailing human bodies, protesting wheels and scurrying marbles sent everything helter-skelter. Mr. Kohl lost his grip, teetered, landed on his bottom. His Fedora, amazingly, stayed on his head. The carriage

Under the Hood

torqued and half-flipped onto one side, both upper wheels spinning. Nan slop-sagged on top of it all.

Buster Keaton would have applauded.

For a flash, Nan saw Mr. Kohl's face, a mere blink's worth, but promising a lifetime of bad dreams. Wrathful black eyes lurked amid wrinkled and darkened leather skin. A fat caterpillar moustache twitched over a darting orange tongue, yellowed teeth, a minimal chin, gray parchment wattle. Immediately the face was lost to shadow.

Mr. Kohl said nothing. He pulled himself up and began to right the perambulator. Nan tried to help. Whether by intent or accident, she caught hold of the black tonneau. It pulled open.

Gotcha.

But.

There was nothing inside. Save a tight dark lining, nothing. Not a thing. After all those months of wondering.

And yet...

Nan's breath solarplexed, she sucked in the night. She buckled under an implosion, a vacuum, a receding of the waters before a tsunami. Her skin goosebumped, her hair polevaulted, her heart sprinted, her bladder threatened to give way.

A cavernous rumble, a volcanic borborygmus. Something unseen rocketed from the pram. A whoosh of chloroform. An explosion of ozone. A whirlwind of darkness. Rough feathers, grating sandpaper, stinging wasps. A surge of mustardy bile, pulsating sheets of glare, vibrating puce, licorice brine propelling up and out in a vortex of cackles, buzzing and screaming high tension wires.

Mr. Kohl had drawn back, a black gargoyle. He didn't speak, but Nan heard a dark scratchy voice in her head.

"*Well, you wanted this, sweetheart. It's all yours.*"

Then he gave her the most malignant gesture she could imagine:

He shrugged.

And the invisible torrent continued to rush from the old perambulator, giving violent birth to new grief, releasing fresh miseries, belching clever ills, spewing contemporary evils into the town, the region, the country—reaching out and out, far, far beyond the neighborhood.

Far, far beyond the insistent curiosity of all those damned neighbors who lived on Pandora Street.

In the Moment

There is one incredible, eternal moment between living and dying when time stops, suspended like a fat, sticky, dewdrop stubbornly hanging from the edge of a petal, reluctant to plummet to oblivion.
In that paradoxical moment of forever-now there are many options. Reviewing your entire life in full detail. Shaping defiant, optimistic plans for conquering leftover desires, old dreams, the unfulfilled. Exploring the sweet and mysterious portals of the yet to be. Learning with exquisite clarity the answers to everything. Or maybe, in a swirling, slow-motion kaleidoscope, wandering through all the options, humming, dancing.
Not yet screaming no, no. No.

Karl wasn't very good at dying. In fact, he had been making quite a mess of it. After being in supreme control his entire adult life, now his mind, his body, his fluids, his very cells were skewed, sliding, seeping, collapsing, taunting, betraying. From revered and feared global CEO, a giant astride the unassailable towers of immense power and enormous wealth, how far, how quickly he had already fallen.
His new world: respirators, tubes, wires, electrodes, monitors, catheters, umbilical horrors. Drip in, drip out.
Absolute command, vigor, pride, arrogance, deceit, indifference, calumny all sagged mutely in sour, coarse sheets, his sweat-sodden monogrammed silk pajamas mocking, mocking.

Now he'd come to his last humiliating seconds, the long-ignored, even sneered-at arrival of the great leveler. His final moment as Karl cum Karl.

Every instant of his childhood tumbled before him. The playmates. The games. The toys. His scruffy, sad-eyed Scottie dog. Sunfilled summers. Secret hideouts. Lewis Carroll, callooh, callay! A giggling little redhead. His grim, often-absent father. A bitter tear. His worn-down mother. Seven maids with seven mops.

Ever: the yearning. Early: the resolve.

High school. Wielding cleverness. Finagling. First kiss. First love. First betrayal. Scholarships. College. Coeds won, coeds cast aside. First job. First promotion. Clawing, cheating to the top. Natural selection. His hero: Darwin. Buyouts, mergers. Good luck, intuitive moves, ruthlessness.

Karl became an opportunist of the first rank.

He soared, triumphed, crushed his enemies, stepped on friends, deceived his wives, alternately ignored and harangued his children. Dined with presidents, bedded starlets, thumbed his nose at the rich, turned his back on the poor. Bought, sold, influenced, manipulated. Laughed at the world and indulged himself in the extreme.

Floating in memory to the smooth voice of Bing Crosby. *The blue of the night.* Delicious young flesh, tropical moons. *The gold of the day.* Endless golf, immaculate greens. Spindrift sailing. In command. Football from the 50-yard line, from the owner's box.

In the Moment

Oh, how happy I would be. Gilt-lined boardrooms and guilt free decisions. Crosby softly whistling, crooning on. *Someone waits for me...*

And what did he still most desire? Eternal youth, eternal life—not possible, even his cartwheeling mind knew that—but one more masterstroke, one more symbol of his near-invincibility, just one more. And it rushed at him as he believed it surely must.

Where there's a will, he chortled, there's a way.

He knew that somewhere close by was a greedy throng, waiting to exult, divide the spoils, spit on his grave. Haha! He could will it all to something or someone absurd, show them who still has the power, even...even then. He'd will everything to an old dogs' home, to the Foreign Legion. Will it all to the society for counting grains of South Seas sand. Oh, frabjous day! Get the damn lawyer!

Bolstered by his plan, emboldened in his forever moment, Karl peered into the infinite—seeking the unambiguous answers he alone was powerful enough to possess.

Ahead, below, above, behind, a glow, a brightness, dazzling but serene. It billowed, enfolded, comforted. Soft voices murmured reassuringly as he slowly tumbled, like Alice, down a radiant and benign tunnel. The answers, he suddenly knew, were in these pearl and coral clouds shimmering before him. Boldly he thought aloud the big questions: What? Why? Who?

Immediately the white glow shredded with a blinding burst of energy, leaving Karl frowning at an infinite mass of gray and black twisting shapes. Agonizing, alarming.
 The more he peered, the more he recognized fragments of his life, coiling and uncoiling. Writhing. Pulsing and repulsing. Flashing through them, flaring with bursts of color, were a myriad shards of missed opportunities. For once, not opportunities for more gain or more power. Quite the opposite.
 He recognized friends he'd spurned, family he'd ignored, kindness he'd sneered at, lives he'd ruined, talents he'd squandered, goodness he'd buried.
 Something clarified and slammed at him like the fierce blue jolts of a defibrillator.
 Karl's mind opened wide, and he gasped at the tangible image of a word he'd always ignored. One small, visceral word with the searing power of lightning: *regret*.
 The word hammered at his ears blinded his eyes tore at his heart. *Regret*.
 Oh, how happy I would be.

There is one incredible moment between living and dying when time stops, suspended...
 How, you ask, could anyone possibly know that?

 Well, I am Karl. This is my story, my life, my reluctant dewdrop, and, oh, now it is sliding, falling, falling...

In the Moment

A final time I force open my eyes, stare from the dark with terrible intensity at my mother, no my wife, no my daughter, no some bland stranger, and compel my cracked lips, my hellish tongue to rasp out the mantra I have learned in my moment of eternity.

"If only...

Charley Horse

They said the kid was Sioux or Cherokee or one of them big brand name Indians. We never knew. But for sure he was a half breed. Half Indian and half sumthun else.

His pa gave him the redman blood. I saw his pa a coupla times down at the feed store. He was a ordinary brave, not a chief or a buckskin warrior, just a skinny guy in a ole checkered shirt, a guy with long shiny black hair. He had a real quiet way about him. Faded, I guess, just like the shirt.

His ma was some white woman from Montana or Missouri or one of them M states. Kinda pretty, kinda blonde and pale, not dark like the brave. When she come into the playground after school, I thought she was pure sunshine arriving. And I liked her pigtails.

The kid's name was Evan Running Horse. Go figure. How would they put that in the phone book? Under R or under H? Guess it wouldn't matter nowadays, as phone books are pert rare. But when we was kids, they still had 'em. Girls walked around with fat ole phone books on their heads, giggling and wiggling in their poodle skirts. Something to do with posturing. Us boys piled phone books on chairs to gain a little height, reach up for things we wasn't supposed to reach for.

Anyway, Evan showed up round the middle of sixth grade. One day our homeroom door opened, the principal shoved him in, said his name. We all laughed and got pert silly till Mr. Roberts shut us up, and that was that.

As far as I know, Evan was the only Indian or near-Indian in the whole doggone school. But he'da stood out in any case. The kid was darn good looking, came out of that baby blender with what I reckon was Indian nobility and the right dash of his mother's prettiness. H<u>e</u> weren't pretty though, he was downright manly handsome even at—what, 13? The rest of us fellas wriggled under our cowlicks and freckles and chubby jowls, and snapped our overall bibs in annoyance. Lookin' at him, we could sense nigh-unbeatable competition down the girl-road even though most of us wasn't anywhere on that road just yet. He'd have had his pick of 'em too, those girls, 'cepting he was Indian after all, and back then, well, some of us kids weren't nowhere near what my mother used to call 'open-minded'.

Evan was smart too, durn it. He didn't shoot his hand up with me-me-me answers like Melissa Kingman or have it made like that egghead Iggy Short, who we always called 'short on the name but long on smarts.' Evan sat in a back corner near the big world globe and didn't stick his hand up at all. But we found out he knew stuff, got the grades, and soon we realized he were competition on the <u>brains</u> road too, even though most of us wasn't on that road either yet, if ever.

I guess we was like every dingdong homeroom, so we had our class bully. He was Dicky Keaton, 14 or so, a kid who had dropped back one grade at least. Dicky was the biggest and bulkiest boy there, an' even though I

Charley Horse

guess you don't have to be big to be a bully, Dicky was a hulker. He was almost as tall as that slickster Elvis Presley who was alllus makin' the girls all squirrelly. But Dicky weren't no Elvis. He had stubby straw hair that poked sideways like yellow barbed wire, eyes two small for his chunky face, and a particular look that mixmastered meanness in with constipation. In short, a fella to avoid.

Well, Evan Running Horse pretty much avoided everyone, except Foureyes Louella Frack, who somehow caught his attention. Maybe coz behind those huge glasses she were too blind to see he was different and treated him like a white boy. (I know that ain't right talk nowadays, but I'm just tellin' it like it was then.)

But Evan coulda hid out in the coat closet all day, and Dicky Keaton woulda still zeroed in on him. It's something in the law of bully nature. Attractive opposites. Yen and yin. Iron filings to a big old magnet. You know what I'm saying.

Dicky took to speaking out of turn to Evan. Torting, taunting—that's the word. He didn't do too much under Mr. Roberts' eye, but in the halls and the playground, Dicky would make crude and rude remarks and gestures. Sometimes he'd kinda bump Evan backwards and one time zinged him on the leg with a slingshot walnut. Which Evan shoulda reported, but never did.

What Dicky liked to do especial was call Evan: Charley Horse. When us kids first learned the Indian's name was Evan Running Horse, we could hear Dicky salivatin' out loud. Didn't take long for the fun to start.

"How ya doin', Charley Horse?" "Hey, Charley Horse, how many scalps ya took today?" Or Dicky'd be yellin' "Oww, a charley horse!" all the while grabbing at his own leg like he had a big cramp. Or leaping about makin' fake Indian war chants and choppin' a pretend tomahawk. Stuff like that.

Dicky had a little group of hang-ons who'd laugh at his clever tricks right on cue and make funny faces at Evan. I still remember 'em. Tom Coolidge, Bobby Wort, and snotty ole Sam Fairburn. Those was the clowns who was Dicky's private posse. They was sort of like them little fish that stay in a shark's good graces by doin' him favors. (I never seen a shark in person, mind you. Thank the Lord for the Discovery Channel. Watchin' it adds two points to yer IQ. Sure makes retirement less borin' too.)

Anyways, you're askin' how Evan took all this bullyin'? I bet you figure sooner or later he'd come out swingin'. Get his own slingshot and shoot back. Or at least call Dicky 'Paleface' or 'Dickybird' or 'Pimplebrain' or something choicer.

But nope. Evan took it all by ignoring it when he could. Or he just stared back at Dicky and his buddies with them dark Indian eyes, givin' them that gila monster gonna-getcha look. Or he'd duck out to the school library where you'd get principalled if you as much as whispered. I saw Evan in there readin' now and then, so maybe it weren't such a bad deal. Sometimes Foureyes Louella'd be there too. But never no bullies.

So here's what finally happened. We was out at recess near the end of the school year, some of us

Charley Horse

workin' up a sweat with dodge ball. Evan's leaning against a tree and just sorta watching the sky.

Dicky starts up his clever remarks. "Hey, Charley Horse, where's your squaw?" "Love that hair, Charley Horse. Did ya know a little dab'll doya?" Brilliant stuff like that. The recess teachers is smoking up in a far corner and don't hear a word, and prob'ly wouldn't do anything if'n they had.

Dicky leaps into a really wild version of his leg cramp routine, jumping like a crazy man. Suddenly we notice he's lots better at it than usual. He's makin' really convincing yell-scream sounds. Dumb Dicky's managed to get hisself a real charley horse this time. It lays him right on the ground, and he's twistin' about like a fat ole snake.

Well, the teachers don't notice or they got Dicky's number and think he's cryin' wolf, so they don't stir. And we stand around watching our favorite bully get his just desserts in spades. That boy was in a-gon-y with a capital E.

But of a sudden, here comes Evan. I figure he's ready to taunt back bigtime, Any number of smartass remarks coulda put the big kebosh on Dicky. We all waited for the grand entertainment. Dicky's squirming and squealing. Pert good fun already.

Only Evan just goes to Dicky, bends down, puts some kinda pressure on the jerk's leg, and before ya could say "Lone Ranger" Dicky's simmerin' down to a small whine and you can tell he's on the mend.

Then Dicky looks up and sees who helped him, and that pimply face goes chalkdust white, the jaw drops and he freezes like he's been zapped by a ray gun. You can hear his five-and-dime brain clickin' in pure puzzlement. It's like a cheap pinball machine dinging. Then he gives a kinda gasp. He cringe-crawls back and scrabbles to his feet. He don't look none at Evan. He just hobbles away, trailed by the Three Stooges.

The year ended with Dicky doin' no more of that particular brand of bullying.

I remember our class photo, took on the schoolyard bleachers maybe the next week. I'm the tall scrawny kid in the back right, the one in the too-big corduroy vest, the one looking like he just ate a rooster. They kept tellin' us to smile, so I was doin' my best.

You wouldn't have no trouble finding Dicky Keaton. He's top middle, looks like he's trying to hold center stage, I guess they call it. Them piggy eyes glare right at yuh. His henchbuddies Tom, Bobby and Sam, are lined up right below him, The four of them all look perty darn sullen. Or maybe it was the sun in their faces.

Well, where'd Evan be, you might wonder. Evan's off in the bottom left corner, down there next to Foureyes Luella Frack. He's almost invisible at first; but when you look closer, there he is. Not smilin', but not sulkin' neither. He's easily the best-looking kid in the photo. That's includin' the girls. And he's sendin' out a certain kind of... confidence. Yeh, confidence, I guess you might call it. I'd a' supposed he'd be showin' loneliness or something like that, but nope, not a hint.

He's looking a bit past the camera, and darned if I don't think that kid has his eye square on the future.

Charley Horse

I think he could see the bloody war many of us boys would be dying in and the tough times ahead for most of us in that backwater school.

But Evan was thinking he'd get through it all, thank you. That kid weren't the outcast we all pegged him for. That kid already knew exactly right who he was.

I believe he figured anyone with a cool name like Evan Running Horse could surely hold his head high and was gonna do just fine.

Cell Block

Here's Mae's problem: at age 78, though otherwise in vigorous good health, still slender and unstooped—after all, she's from deep-rooted Idaho stock—her mind seems to be unraveling, bit by bit. She finds herself grasping at memories, agonizing over failures of recall, worrying that whatever afflicted her mother decades ago has now awakened and is slowly uncoiling in her brain.

Some memories are bold, oddly-fresh and vivid, while others are faded and blurred. It's glum, chum. Dumb.

These days unasked-for rhymes dance around her, amusing and annoying. Cloying, toying.

The doctors have no easy answers. Perhaps a dementia. Maybe Alzheimer's, Mrs. Tolliver. We can't be sure. They fall back on that popular mantra, too-soon-to-tell. Tell, swell. Hell.

At least Mae and her husband can laugh about it. Sometimes. They heard the only way to confirm Alzheimer's is post-mortem, dissecting brain tissue. "I'm sorry," Mae smiles with unwrinkled radiance, "but I need every cell. Especially now. No autopsy, no cutting, thank you." Cutting, tut-tutting. Rutting. Where did that come from? she wonders.

Mae's not been sleeping well either. And now there's this wandering thing.

Many a summer morning, Henry still dozing, Mae stands at their small kitchen window and looks up at the tawny Boise foothills. The dawn sun paints the rim rock. The shadows move, the dark rough edges shift into astonishing shapes, impossible animals, jagged demons.

Below those sandstone ridges is the Old Idaho Penitentiary, the biggest puzzle in Mae's slowly-reassembling life. This summer, for some reason, she is strongly drawn to the prison. She wanders over there, sometimes cognizant she's doing it, other times finding herself in the cool confines of the women's building, not recalling the journey.

It's an easy walk. Mae can go out the back door of their red brick cottage, open the garden gate, step onto the trail, cut through Quarry Park and the adjoining fields and soon be at the massive outer sandstone wall of the Women's Ward, which sits at right angles to the penitentiary proper. Not that the penitentiary was ever proper, she thinks—a hundred years of anguish, guilt, fear, toil and death. History tries to put a dusty haze on it all, but she can almost feel it. Haze, glaze, maze.

Why does she need to go there, she wonders? Why does she step through the fortified doorway—conveniently open for tourists—cross the scruffy garden with its forlorn rose bushes, and slip into the dim prison building with its seven barred cells, its poignant photographs and stories of women long lost? Bossed. Tossed. At what cost?

Henry sometimes finds Mae sitting on the long wooden bench under the thick-barred central skylight, or standing motionless in one of the small side rooms, or leaning on the coarse metal grating of a cell, staring in. She simply doesn't know why she's there.

Cell Block

The family has started discussions. The most worried is Samantha, their daughter, who theorizes a long maternal line of dementia. Sam's grandmother, her great aunt and her mother's sister all had mental issues of one sort of another. Nuts, she thinks, but never voices that word. She fears she's the heir apparent.

Sam tries to focus on Mae's wandering. "Maybe it's that damn Lady Bluebeard," she says, twisting strands of her long black hair.

"You think Mom identifies with a serial killer?" scoffs their son Frank. "She wouldn't hurt a fly." He doesn't say this with any admiration.

"What about those coincidences?" Sam persists.

Years ago, taking a tour of the Women's Ward, Mae and Henry discovered that Prisoner 3052, Lyda Southard, the infamous husband-poisoner, shared Mae's birth names, Anna Mae. And 3052 was the phone number of the farm where Mae grew up.

"How bizarre is that?" said Mae, scrutinizing Southard's face, hunting for—what, she wasn't sure. The prisoner stared bemusedly into the camera, looking almost pretty, not very penal.

The family is still discussing Mae's wandering. Sam's husband suggests that Mae is attracted by the huge lighted cross hovering on Table Rock above the penitentiary. He proposes the cross is a steeple, the Women's Ward a cathedral.

""Moth to the holy flame," he says. "So what if Mae's never been religious? She's at the age when people turn to God."

"If that's true, I sure hope she's not required to go to prison to meet Him," says Henry, mildly.

Mae's condition concerns the family, but apart from her wandering, oddities of speech and memory quirks, she functions fairly normally. Everyone's happy she's spending much of this summer in her garden, nursing vegetables, tending roses.

One rose in particular, a hybrid with complex, fiery blooms, draws Mae's attention. She loves touching the supple petals, relishes smelling the buttery musk, contemplating the intricate layers, orange and red.

Red was her mother's favorite color. Belle always wore something red. A cherry dress, a scarlet sash, a ruby hat, a pair of crimson gloves. You could spot Belle far out in the pasture, brilliantly aflame amid the dusty greens and browns.

In contrast, Mae's Dad, Charlie, a quiet man always quietly attired, was a genius at blending into the landscape, right up to the day the tractor accident made him part of that landscape forever.

Even as Belle lost more and more of her always-frail grip on reality—and Charlie's death sped that along—she constantly wore red, clinging to her defiant signature.

Mae thinks of Aunt Ada, Belle's sister, always in black, her long dark hair in a very tight bun. Belle and Ada. Rouge et noir. They'll go far. Har har. Mae frowns at the rhyming.

After Ada married Uncle Snapper, Ada supposedly panicked on their wedding night—did he snap at her?

Cell Block

They didn't stay married long. Ada soon holed up in the Idanha Hotel, living under one of the curious turrets. She rarely came out. Dear Aunt Ada, trailing a whispery aroma of cinnamon and the past.

Uncle Snapper surely earned his nickname, Mae thought, from his protruding jaw. It thrust absurdly forward, the prow of a dugout canoe. What was his real name? Arlon, Arlie, Arlington, yes. Arlington Davis. After Charlie's death, because of Belle's diminishing capacities, Arlington leased and ran the farm. He was good at it, keeping things going until he retired and the first of their land selloffs began.

Thinking of the farm tugs Mae back into the hayloft, the summer Dad died, where she lost her virginity to a young man—no, a boy, really—about to be shipped off to the police action in Korea. She can't recall his name. But she remembers the soft scratchiness tickling her back, the low laughter, the swell of desire, the peculiar mingling of pleasure and pain. She remembers rolling to the side and seeing a wide-eyed mouse staring at her, a complicit sister. Gorgeous eyes, that mouse.

And Wayne—yes, that was his name, Wayne! Pain, slain—Wayne donned a splendid uniform, proudly departed for Korea and promptly got himself killed. Then there was...

A breeze blows the rose sideways. Mae blinks, her reverie disturbed.

Henry is doing volunteer work at the food bank. Mae freshens up, decides to eat a half sandwich and a candy bar. My last meal, she muses, then wonders why she would think that.

Nibbling her food, she glances out the window. The foothills are sere and golden.

She steps into the back garden, filled with thriving vegetables. Each bed has signs identifying the plants. A carryover from her library career. Always lining things up, everything in its place. The system, what was it called? Duty? Dewey. Yes, Dewey decimal system, Admiral Dewey, Huey, Dewy, and Louie. She giggles. I'm so screwy.

She notices the spreading broccoli. "Hey! You're crowding out the baby squash. Read the sign: B-A-B-Y!" She turns to find her gardening gloves. But suddenly there's something else to do. She has to go. Immediately.

She unlocks the garden gate and walks toward the penitentiary, her fine white hair aglow, ruffling in the afternoon breeze.

Grasshoppers leap ahead of her. Mae thinks of the Mormon crickets her Dad would take her to watch, the creatures swarming across the country lanes, jiggling rivers of oily black, peppered with reds, purples, greens. Something fun to share if I have ever have kids.

If I ever have kids. God, she clearly remembers thinking that so many decades ago. What else? But other memories bolt. Even my own brain denies me, she thinks, my own mind keeps secrets from me. Secrets. Regrets. Egrets.

Two white dogs scampering through the grass in front of her have transformed into lovely white birds. Mae is filled with delight, but a burst of barking brings her back. In moments she's by the high, worn stone prison walls.

Cell Block

The place seems almost welcoming. Mae stops at the outer gate and touches the dirty tan surface of the wall. It's rough, gritty, yet improbably soft.

Tourists burst out, waving camera phones, making jokes. As Mae walks through the small garden, she feels depressed at the irreverence of such people. This isn't a shrine—no, not a shrine, fine, mine—but it deserves something, maybe respect. It has meaning. Meaning. Greening. Oh, these roses need attention.

Mae is fairly tall, but several of the rose bushes dwarf her, reach long straggly arms down toward her. Could Lyda Mae have planted these? Lyda Mae, Lida Rose. So long ago, who's to know? Go, now go. Lida Rose, I'm home again.

Mae enters the squat, cheerless building. Once more she feels as though she should be here to... Her mind rebels. She walks to the first barred cell, puts her hand on flat grimy steel and peers through the gray slats into the shadowy recesses. A tiny space, sagging bunk bed, miserable toilet, small grilled window, yellow glare beyond.

Escape. You want to escape, don't you ladies? Lyda Anna Mae, you escaped, didn't you? I needed to escape.

Mae was smart, and college and a professional career were her way off the farm, though many years later, with Belle dead, Uncle Snapper retired and the property much smaller, Mae convinced Henry they should return to live in the farmhouse.

Her mind takes her there now, and, oh, there's the barn, and the hayloft and Wayne breathing softly in Mae's ear, promising wild huckleberries for breakfast, and they lived happily ever after, and Grace Rose was with them. And. And.

Mae Day. Mae Day.

Her memories buck violently and throw her back into a puzzled present. She drops her hand from the grating, and turns to look for Henry, who at this moment is crossing into the stale shade of the prison.

"You OK?" he asks.

"I had a thought," she tells him. "But it's gone." Mae Day.

After supper, Mae is her old self. They sit on the back patio and savor the warm, sweet grassiness of a slow summer evening, drink tart lemonade, and watch ravens lazily hunt for thermals.

"It fascinates me how the inmates quarried sandstone and built much of the penitentiary themselves." Mae said. "I wonder if my mind has done that, built my own prison, locked secrets inside."

"Hm. That's possible," says Henry, scratching at mosquito bite. "But what secrets could you have, Mae? They'd need to be pretty serious for your brain to do this."

"Let's face it, these days my brain is highly suspect."

"You're doing great, Babe."

"But one minute I'm me, here, and the next my memory's off on a wild goose chase. It's frustrating. Scary, hairy. And those stupid rhymes haunt me. Haunt, taunt. Whoops! It's become a habit, rabbit. See what I mean?" The trademark Mae Tolliver giggle floats into the air.

Henry lights his pipe. "Can I suggest something?" A puff. "Just a small theory."

"Sure." A whiff of cherry tobacco draws Mae back to the early years of their marriage, when she'd moved eons away from the traumas of her teens.

Henry takes another puff. "I wonder if you're beating up on yourself because we sold the farm. Could your subconscious feel guilt, think you need to be punished?"

Mae smiles. She loves it when Henry's usual linear thinking gives way to insight.

She muses, half to herself. "That's possible. But I don't think it's the land, even though I do feel guilty about all the development. It could be something else that my mind's locked up in the slammer, in solitary."

Henry chuckles. "Well, not to worry," he says. "Just feed it bread and water and leave it there."

They sit contentedly, take pleasure in the rising of the ghostly summer moon, the crickets singing.

The next day Mae decides to bake a surprise for Henry. Sticky buns, she thinks. She bustles about the kitchen, pulling out bowls, spoons, flour, sugar. She opens the spice drawer. Everything's carefully labeled, stored alphabetically. "Once a librarian, always a librarian," she tells the fragrant yellow roses joyous in a heavy green vase. "Librarian... Marion... Carry on!"

Humming, she selects a new jar of cinnamon, rests it on the counter, crackles the plastic ring, opens the lid, shakes out a spoonful.

The synaptic leap is palpable. Aunt Ada is comforting, counseling, sure of herself, no hint of old maid except her feathery aura of cinnamon and must, Aunt Ada is taking care of things with such efficiency and grace. Oh, Grace, my dear little Grace Rose.

And the bars swing open, Mae remembers the baby she gave up, Wayne's child, rosebud pink, barely seen but instantly named, and crazy ancient Aunt Ada, Rapunzel come down from her tower, kind, understanding, arranging.

Spilling the cinnamon, Mae weeps for Ada, loving, sobs for Daddy, crushed, Belle, drifting, Wayne, killed, for the impossible decision, for Grace Rose, gone, gone. Done, done. Spilt, quilt. Guilt. No wonder I seek a place of shame. Shame, blame.

She's ashamed, too, that she's never told Henry. She meant to tell him, then life moved so away from those difficult years, and her secret slid into an old chest of memories, locked and hidden away.

Could she tell Henry now? Perhaps he needs to know, she thinks, before my flippery slippery mind disintegrates more, before it slips into a fragmented world and I can't come back.

Mae slowly collects the spilled cinnamon, stands there, inhaling the velvety scent of roses, citrus and fern, love and loss.

That afternoon, she walks through the fields, stands for a moment outside the lumpy sandstone wall, enters the modest garden before the Women's Ward.

She crosses to a stubborn old rosebush with smoky purple blooms. The largest blossom greets her with a warm fragrance, honey and anise. Mae puts on her well-worn red gloves, pulls out her favorite clippers, and begins to prune the plant, carefully, lovingly.

Grace Rose, I hope you are alive, and happy. And free. Free. Be. Me.

Mae pauses, looks up from her pruning, surveys the prison garden.

There is much to be done.

Loch Ness Monsters

"Please, Sylvia, give me a moment to think."

The winds attacked the cottage, sweeping down from the highlands like clansmen on a suicide raid. The whine of aeolian bagpipes skirled about us, gusts raping the eaves, pillaging the chimney pots, racing through cracks in the walls, keening, keening. I felt defenseless. The weather was the least of it.

"All right. You've had your moment, Edgar." Was she being metaphorical? Cynical? You never could tell with Sylvia. She slammed down her cup, chipping the Wedgewood saucer and sloshing tea onto Mrs. McNaughton's embroidered placemat. A brief staccato of quirky Scottish rain lashed the window. Rain this minute, sun the next. Here you never knew, even in mid-August.

The panes rattled. Sylvia flicked a crumb of shortbread into oblivion and stared at me.

'I'll repeat the question."

Of course she'd repeat it. She always did. She'd already asked twice.

I studied the parlor's biggest painting, a gloomy oil of Bonnie Prince Charlie fleeing to Skye in a small battered boat. Should you run from failure or face it head on?

"I need three, no, four more days."

"For what? To think about it or to actually head back to New York?"

The wan daylight dropped to a subterranean low. The glow from the table lamp cringed, not up to the task. The room huddled in dreariness. Ordinarily I wouldn't mind. My thoughts would be off seeking inspiration for my next symphony. Off in the worried clouds hovering between sun and loch, in the aspen leaves fluttering furiously, in the ash trees bending in obeisance to whatever roamed the dark waters. But at present, my dear young wife was nagging. I had to stop her.

"I mean when we could depart. I need four more days. Minimum."

"Oh, fine. I knew an open-ended trip was a dumb idea. And next time we take solo sabbaticals."

Sylvia sat down abruptly, the overstuffed tartan armchair wheezing, the dingy antimacassar fluttering. Instantly, the wind dropped. Perfect synchrony always interests me.

'It's not that I don't think your work's important, Edgar." She didn't. "Or that I think this is a wild goose chase." She did. "It's just that it's time to go home." Home, especially to her current lover. When you marry a younger woman, extra bees soon tend to buzz around.

The windows clattered. I imagined saurian claws tap-dancing on the panes. I liked rain, especially the sounds it made. And here it kept the clouds of attacking midges at bay.

My nose twitched. The reek of peat. Wood smoke. Something briny and not altogether pleasant. I looked at Sylvia slumped in the chair, and I felt a tiny touch of guilt.

Loch Ness Monsters

"Tell you what," I offered. "Let's drive up to Inverness this evening. Have a few drinks. Splurge on a nice dinner at Kingsmills or The Williamson Arms. It's too windy for my night excursion. I'll put that off."

The ever-surprising Scottish sun thrust a golden shaft into the room. Sylvia turned yellow, a gorse bush. And just as prickly. "All right. Anyplace besides that boring village pub. If I have to face another Scotch egg, I'll jump into the loch."

The wind resumed howling, soon in a discordant duel with the howls and moans of real bagpipes. Mrs. McNaughton's tin-eared nephew Angus liked to practice in the adjacent cottage. Angus was not Julliard material. Yesterday he strutted outside in full tartan regalia—kilt, sporran and a silver dagger at one knee—planted his stout legs in the onion bed and blasted away. No wonder the Loch Ness monster preferred to stay underwater.

"Creepy little man," said Sylvia. "I think he spies on us."

"He's just another would-be swain, Sylvia." 'Swain' is a more interesting word than 'admirer'. I first noticed it when I was writing choral variations on a Shakespeare poem, 'Who is Sylvia?' These days that was the question.

The armchair groaned. Sylvia pushed herself up. A small puff of lavender talcum whispered from the cushion. Sylvia sniffed. "Look, can we go for that drink soon?"

The fickle skies had cleared. We sped up the Great Glen toward the city of Inverness. Sylvia drove, freeing me to scan the loch. She didn't drive out of kindness. It was self-preservation. Our first day here, with me driving and rubbernecking, we came close twice to taking the plunge and once to careening into a flock of sheep. Mutton is not my favorite dish.

Loch Ness was on our left, beckoning, yet a little menacing. The black waters lapped close to the narrow road. The erratic sun bounced silvergold dots off the wave tops. The loch was a dark music score, ripples for the staff, lightglints as notes. I sensed a reel, then a dirge.

The Scottish paradox. Gaiety and dourness paired, the highland fling and tribal sadness wrapped into one. As a descendent of Scottish immigrants, I had murky depths in my blood.

"Hard to think it's pushing a thousand feet deep," I mused aloud.

"Well, actually it's 230.7 meters." Math professors love to be precise. Sylvia could work any number to an infinite decimal point. Spot on accuracy. Except when she tried to add up the elements of real life. of marriage. There she was prone to errors.

She made another fast calculation. "That would be about 757 feet." Was she rubbing it in?

"Give or take." My benign tone surprised me. "Regardless, it's a precipitous drop starting almost at the shoreline."

"Hmm." She dared a glance at the loch. "God, I hope the salmon they serve around here doesn't come from that black hole."

An osprey rose a few yards offshore, flew leisurely toward the nearest trees. Its talons gripped a still-

Loch Ness Monsters

wriggling fish, bloodied silver. Someone's dinner indeed came from Loch Ness.

Weathered fishing boats tried their luck, masts dancing to a lively tempo. A tourist boat, festooned with blue and red pennants, hunted for Nessie. I looked across at the stubborn remains of Urquhart Castle, its tower a jagged silhouette against the soft-sloped hills. The partial ruins had stood for centuries. Some things go completely to ruin much faster than others.

With no warning, a giant silent shadow raced straight at us, darkened the road, climbed the windshield, passed overhead. We both ducked. After the fact. Behind us, sudden thunder in a rapid diminuendo.

Sylvia did a great job of not driving us into the loch. "What the hell was that?" she said.

"Some flying cousin of Nessie?" I ventured. "A pterodac—"

"Get serious."

"But it's more likely the Royal Air Force at play."

"Then it's royally stupid. God, I feel safer in Central Park. When can we get that drink?"

At Inverness, we sat on a smooth oak bench in a back corner of a Church Street pub, far from the door, far from the wind and, for the moment, far from dissention. The room hummed with conversation, pulsed to the cheery sparkle of a radio dance band. My foot tapped. I could make out accordions, Shetland fiddles, familiar Scottish tunes. The odors of fish and chips, strong ale and wet tweed swirled about us.

Sylvia's drink soon began to mellow her. On our first evening in the highlands she'd discovered the shandy, a peculiar concoction combining beer and ginger ale, fortified with vodka. She chugged one of those now, alternating workman-size gulps with ladylike sips of a Glenfiddich single malt. I wasn't about to remark on the oddity of that pairing. A relaxed Sylvia remained a reasonably-good companion. I gave happy attention to my own gin and bitter lemon. I can handle bitterness when it's in the confines of a tumbler.

"So, Edgar." Sylvia ran a finger along the rim of her shandy glass. She managed a low wet squelch. "So, are you getting what you want?"

"What I want?" There she was again with double meanings.

"Want from this trip."

My tapping foot performed a sidestep. "Are you? Getting what you want?"

She raised the glass and studied me through amber. "Scotland's lovely, the lake's interesting, your mythic monster is—monastery. But I'm ready for home. Yep, I'm ready-teddy."

"I don't think of Nessie as a monster. Quite the opposite. It's more a philosophical construct."

"Edgar, darling, don't be so obtude, ob, obtuse." I hated being called 'darling'. "And don't be boring. I don't like it when you're pedattic, pendantish, whatever. Look, would you get me another shandy? There's a good boy."

I elbowed through some mug-wielding rowdies and ordered Sylvia's drink. I asked the bartender to leave out the vodka, double the ginger ale.

During the school year, Sylvia tried to limit her drinking. She wanted to be sharp for her students. "Calculus plus too much liquor equals insolvable problems," she told me. But her summers, she said, were a time for letting loose. Henry in the Catskills, Kurt in Paris and now Whatshisname in New York. Those were letting loose. My trained ear wasn't expert at hearing undertones for nothing.

The crowd at the bar cheered at televised soccer. I hipchecked back to our table. Sylvia savored the first slog, thumped down the glass.

"So. Music and monsters. Tell me again. In plain English. Well, plain schottische, Scottish. Why're we here? Why aren't you home writing Beethoven's Fifth?" A giggle "His Fifth of Scotch?" Another giggle. She leaned toward me. "Why d'ya have the hots for Nessie, Ludwig?"

I sipped my gin and said nothing.

A classical composer and a mathematics professor and would seem a likely match. A common interest in precision and interworking components. That sort of thing. But Sylvia rarely seemed to grasp the intangibles which went into my music. The metaphysical. The mysterious. None of that comes from the mathematical side. The soul seeks much more. Either you get that or you don't. Sylvia didn't. It never used to bother me. I thought I could teach her. I was wrong.

The pub, more and more crowded, vibrated with boozy enthusiasm counterpointed by the thwacks of a darts game. Leaning closer, Sylvia tried to nudge me out of my thoughts. She breathed whisky and beer into my face. Chanel number something teased my nostrils with sandalwood. Despite the ruckus, I could hear her heartbeat. Her sultriness was almost arousing.

I'd never questioned why I'd fallen for her, pursued her despite our substantial age difference. Brainy, often funny, asymmetrically beautiful, definitely sexy. She had a musical laugh. And she liked Mozart, Brahms, Rachmaninoff.

Not long after we married, she engaged me in an amazing discussion of mathematical certainties in the music of Bach. I had the feeling she was far ahead of me. There was much she understood about music.

But understand me she did less and less. The harmony prevalent early in our relationship now too often slid toward dissonance. After only five years of marriage, our June-November pairing was in a marked decrescendo.

She was more or less sober by the time we sat down to dinner at the venerable Williamson Arms. The dark paneled walls displayed 19th century hunting and fishing lithographs. The room exhaled primeval oxtail soup and fresh linseed oil. The highback chairs were stiff, unyielding. My seat cushion scratched and poked.

Service was obsequious with just a hint of Scottish cheekiness. Stream-caught trout for madam. For the gent, the chicken with whisky-soaked haggis. A deft choice, sir. Or did he say daft?

"Haggis?" Sylvia raised her eyebrows and her voice. "Becoming daring in your old age, are you, darling?"

I eyed the wine list. "Isn't daring my norm?"

She smiled. "Will you work haggis into your symphony?"

"I'll take that as a serious question. And the serious answer is yes, in the general way anything about the highlands will influence the score."

"How about making it the title? Edgar Crannoch's Symphony Number Four, "The Haggis". It has a certain, oh, animal pull to it."

I chuckled. I don't know why I responded so mildly. Lately Sylvia the Playful had been masking Sylvia the Barb-slinger. She was good at that. Masking. Slinging.

"If we stay in Britain long enough," she sighed, a sudden coquette, "it might even become Sir Edgar Crannoch."

I bit into a miniature scone drizzled with cheese. The thing rasped under my tongue, a gritty ball of bile-ish flour.

"Message received, Sylvia. We'll get you home soon enough."

"In the meantime...?"

"Look, earlier you asked 'why Nessie?' I'm not on the hunt for some prehistoric creature. Not at all. Whether or not there's a Loch Ness monster isn't the question."

"What is?"

"Let me finish. Please."

She gave me an irritatingly-obedient nod. Sometimes she treated me as though I were her father. I pushed back a scowl.

"I'm trying to soak up the essence of this place. To experience it intuitively so I can infuse my symphony with it. Make the music deeply evocative for the sensitive listener."

"How about for us clods?"

"Sorry. I'm being pedantic again. Let's just say I want the symphony to give listeners a feeling of being immersed in the highlands. And since Nessie—real or not—is a presence here, a sense of the monster will make it into the work. Somehow."

"Godzilla in the French horns?" She had the grace to blanch at my aggrieved look. "I'm sorry, Edgar. I think I understand. You want nothing overt, but lots of subtext that really gets to us."

I nodded. Sylvia knew darn well what I hoped to do. She also knew how to push my buttons, battered old dance accordion that I was.

"Ah well," she said, "no matter what, this trip's a fine tax write-off. For both of us."

"For you? Since when?"

"Since yesterday. I'm researching a Scottish mathematician, Sir Thomas Muir. Might give a lecture on the old boy."

"What gave you that idea?"

"I found a book about Muir in the parlor. Turns out he was a pal of Mrs. McNaughton's grandfather. What more could I ask?"

Mrs. McNaughton was our landlady pro tem. Full of talk. Full of advice. On our first morning here, Mrs. McNaughton, her face ruddy and beaming, her substantial bosom steadying a big floral tray, had served us our 'proper Scottish breakfast'—far too much of everything, including lumpy porridge and overdone kippers—then lingered to confer wisdom.

"Now, I know ye'll be wanting to go looking for Nessie." She didn't wait for an answer. "Mind you be very careful on the edge of the loch. Verra, verra careful." I loved the way she rolled her r's.

Sylvia assumed a schoolgirl's face. "Will the monster lunge up and grab us?"

"Och, no, pet. But the banks are muckle slippery. The loch's cold and deadly. It's no for swimming. Poor wee Jimmy Henderson drowned just up the way this very summer. And they never found Sheila Campbell last spring. Things vanish in oor loch. And—well, just be very careful."

"I can't swim anyway," said Sylvia, "so there's no danger I'll be going out there."

"That's just as well, pet."

"Have you ever seen Nessie?" Sylvia was leading the poor woman on. I wasn't the only person she toyed with.

"Aye. It's a sight to give ye a quiver. I've watched Nessie off the castle several times, a wee bit far out. An' once I was on the bike by the shore, peddling home at eventide, and there the beastie was. As near as my sister's house next door and almost as big. Slippery-shiny and dripping boggy water all over. A big dragony thing but without the fire. When it saw me, it gang under the loch quicker than two shakes of a lamb's tail."

"She makes that stuff up for tourists," Sylvia said, cutting her trout. The Williamson used real fish knives. I hadn't seen one in years. "All the locals make up Nessie stories. I don't really fault them, though. Do you?"

"Life's full of big lies and little lies." I toyed with my food. "Lies. Illusions. Deception. Some of it doesn't matter. Some of it's useful. Some of it..."

"My God, what's in your haggis? Scotch weed? Don't go off the deep end, Edgar. Especially not around Loch Ness." Playful Sylvia again. Or was that a parry?

The Williamson had become over-warm and stuffy. We gobbled the last of a nutty local brie, gulped our port and went outside. A few years ago we would have strolled arm in arm, hip to hip. Tonight, I took the high road and she took the low road. If that phrase means not being in sync, it's the right one.

Our car was several streets over. I spotted a shortcut, an alley guarded by two cracked and leaning bollards. We stepped between them and found ourselves on cobblestones. Sylvia shrugged and strode ahead. Her heels clipclopped in 2/2 time. At any moment I expected her to twist an ankle. My footing wasn't much better.

We crossed through a pocket of stagnant odors. Urine, rotten eggs, and what might have been a rancid dead rat. Sylvia winced.

"Breathe deeply," I said. "It's just right for my evocative music." Who was I discounting? Her or me?

A skinny ginger cat, yowling a piercing F sharp, emerged from a pile of debris, saw us, stood in our path. Angry hazel eyes. Nasty cerise scar slashing down one marmalade cheek. The tail swished side to side, a feline metronome.

Something flashed out in front of us. Glass shattered across the cobbles. The cat fled. Laughter.

Loch Ness Monsters

Three young men lurched out of a close. Bright blue and red football scarves flopped over drab working clothes. Grimy woolen caps thrust back, insolent. Hooligans. A Scottish specialty.
"Ye'll never get ay pussy that way, Col." Laughter. "Ye've got to sneak up on it like, flash yer charms." Snickers.
The three watched the cat. They hadn't yet seen us. Sylvia took my hand. First time in months. We edged backwards. Quietly.
The tallest swiveled, a redheaded cobra coiling.
"Fuck me. Look here, lads."
He flipped down his cigarette. Sparks bounced across the cobblestones. The others turned. An unholy trio.
The squatty blond winked at Sylvia and aimed a thumb at me. "Is this yer pa, sweetheart? Och, she can do better. Aye, Wullie?"
Wullie, gaunt and tubercular, rubbed his crotch and grunted something, a garbage disposal grinding in his throat. He bared yellow teeth.
We backed up. I could hear Sylvia breathing hard. Her perfume, her sweat and her fear clung to me.
"Whit de ye think, Ferg?" The tall one slowly pulled the ends of his scarf, toweled his neck.
Ferg, his face a battlefield of acne and rosacea, licked his fat lips.
"It's na a time fer thinkin', Col. It's time for humpin' while the iron's hot, eh?"
Col hooted. "Aye, an my iron's hot indeed, lads." Wullie hiccupped a snigger.

Ferg took a step towards us. "Fancy a wee squeeze, lass? Geeze a hump?"

He pointed at me. "An you, you auld jobbie-jabber. Get out yer wallet. Hafta pay to watch the show, eh?"

Wullie growled something which sounded like "Aye, pay up."

Behind them, two more louts appeared, sauntering up the alley. Burly and Burlier. My breath faltered. My bladder misbehaved.

Col sensed the newcomers and turned.

"Scram it, ye willywallys. This pair o' pigeons is oors." He noticed their green and yellow scarves. "Oh shite! A coupla weegies, is it? A brace 'o Celtics."

"Ach, git back to Glasgy!" snarled Ferg, dropping into a boxer's stance. Wullie hawked and spat.

"Oh-ho, look, Donnie," said Burly, tossing a scarf end over his shoulder. "Invershnecky idyuts."

"Aye." Donnie cracked his knuckles. "Thistle Jessies right enough."

"Gae back to Glasgy, ye hamshanks," Col said, "And take yer puddock Celtics wi ya."

Ferg chimed in. "Them clagtails couldn't find a fitba if it was up their arse."

"Oh yeh?" jeered Burly. "Thistles, are ye? Thistles hae naught but wee pricks, eh?"

The verbal melee intensified. They shuffled closer to each other. We'd been forgotten. Sylvia had the presence of mind to slip off her shoes. We retreated to the main road and took the long route to our car.

"Are you all right? I asked.

"Of course. So that's what it's like to be saved by knight errants?"

"Knights hooligan, I think."

"I liked the green scarves."

"Hope they get hung up by them. By the balls."

"Oh, Edgar. You're just sorry my knight wasn't you." Sylvia had perfected the art of rubbing it in.

As we drove back along the loch, now with me at the wheel, she sat silently for some time. Then she began to sing, in a very passable alto. I recognized an old Scots lament.

I've seen the smiling of fortune beguiling;
tasted her pleasures, and felt her decay.
Sweet is her blessing, so kind her caressing;
but now they are fled, and fled far away.

"That was lovely," I said, meaning it. "You surprise me."

"Well, you don't know everything about me, Edgar. Do you?"

The sky was seductive. Ambers, mauves, pinks. The sun seemed reluctant to set. Clouds flirted with the hills. The blueblack loch was tranquil and somber.

"Look, I've changed my mind," I said. "I think I will do that walkabout tonight after all, inhale the gloaming, intuit the lurking monster, that sort of thing."

"Oh?"

"This next symphony's got to be right. It's important. It's vital. Apart from the needs of my ego, I don't want commissions drying up. I don't want to go back to full time teaching. Julliard will survive without me."

"Still smarting over your last one? I thought it had many good things about it. Lots."

"You know damn well it lacked my old brilliance. Same with my last film score and the chamber works. Not up to snuff. A creative lull." Ideally I was not on a downhill slide into hack. I kept that concern to myself.

"Pity they don't sell insurance for creative lulls. Better yet, insurance against failed symphonies. You could've bought some of that when we took out our life insurance policies."

"Very funny. But I don't intend any more works to fail."

"Maybe you could even get the insurance as a rider on our..."

"Sylvia..."

The remainder of the drive south was in silence. Sylvia watched ducks skimming the water. My mind was creatively busy. I envisioned a huge Nessie surging up, prying off the top of the car, lifting Sylvia out and taking her away, my wife wriggling like a salmon, screaming like Faye Wray in the grasp of her gorilla lover. This image wouldn't figure in my new symphony, but the action surely would prompt me to write my best film score ever.

As we entered our half of the cottage, I smelled vestiges of fried sausage, burnt toast and something I couldn't identify. Sylvia wrinkled her nose.

"I think I'll find a little reading matter," she said. "And maybe the brandy."

I found my boots and a vest. Hunted for a pocket flashlight. Dug out a notebook to record my inspirations. If I still had such things.

"That nasty little man." Sylvia burst back into the parlor. I was sitting in the talcum-puffing chair pulling on my boots.

"Who? Thomas Muir?" I saw the math prof's biography in her hand.

"Don't be ridiculous. Andy. Angus. Whatever his name is. The tubby jerk next door. I think he's been through my things."

"How do you know?"

"It's a feeling. A sense. Something in the wardrobe isn't quite the same. I dunno. There's also a mustier smell."

"Like farty old bagpipes?"

"You're joking, but that's almost it. That and stale cigarettes. And the other night I thought I saw him skulking in the yard, trying to see in."

"We could talk with Mrs. McNaughton, but it's a little delicate."

"Too bad. I want to bring it up tomorrow anyway." Sylvia paced, thwacking Dr. Muir on her thigh. I hoped he was enjoying it.

She stopped mid-stride. "Would you mind if I come along tonight? I don't want to sit here alone. I promise to be quiet so you can absorb things or meditate or whatever you'll be doing out there." She never missed a chance for a dig.

"What I'll be doing is walking around for a few hours. Observing the changing light, Experiencing the end of day over the loch. Listening, feeling. Maybe making a few notes. And yes, absorbing. If that's OK, sure, come along."

Soon we were walking towards the loch. An owl hooted, the high repeated A Flat announcing our intrusion. Creatures rustled in the shrubbery. Something crunched in the woods. A red squirrel, chattering, shot up a pine, pursued by a marten, flashing chocolate and apricot, ironic colors for death. Fortunately, no chubby voyeur in kilts seemed to be stalking us.

Then came the attack. We'd forgotten about the midges, tiny piranhas of the air, cousins to our own no-see-ums. As we rustled through a damp grassy sward, they arose to savage us.

"Put these buggers in your damn music," said Sylvia, swatting. "Evocative, my ass."

A breeze came to the rescue, spinning the biting horde away, bringing a brackish tang and a hint of wild roses.

Behind us, the super full moon was rising, pure and stately, a pale whole note taking stage in the eastern sky.

We walked over a small rise guarded by stands of silver birch, zigzagged down into a field strewn with tiny wildflowers, stepped along a muddy, boot-sucking trail, and were stopped by the weed-fringed edge of the loch.

Loch Ness Monsters

Close to the water was a narrow path of pebbles and tramped-down dirt. We went north. Now and then we had to skirt a defiant shrub growing near the edge, unruly branches drooping over the black water.

Slowly the sun relaxed into twilight. The surface of the loch was gunpowder floating in ink. Tiny syncopated wavelets, hypnotic, slapped the shore.

Clouds stretched, thinned, wove strands of silver and orange, blossomed, enflamed. The sun dropped mutely behind the ancient hills, two gold-red rays upthrust, arms in benediction.

Dusk. The dark symphony of the loch enveloped me. Peace. And a harmony I'd not felt in a long time.

All this was what I'd been seeking. What I could hope to reflect in my music. To redeem my career.

A piper began playing on the opposite shore. Melancholy notes glided over the water, small lost birds. Soulful, perfect.

"My God! Look at that." Sylvia shattered the moment.

I'd forgotten her. And she'd forgotten her promise of silence.

"Out there. To the left." She pointed. "Is that a deer?" Some sort of animal was struggling to swim west, its head slowly bobbing.

I saw a long ripple crease the surface—a bore tide, a seiche, shifting cloud shadows, I couldn't tell. The waters around the deer darkened. I squinted. The animal vanished.

"Oh!" Sylvia cried out. "Did you see that?"

I half-turned toward her. A bad mistake. A weed, a root, a troll caught my leg. I twisted, slipped on the scree, grabbed at a thorny branch, stutter-splashed into the loch.

Ice knifed around my ankles, razored up my legs. Despite the barbs, my left hand still held on to the overhanging shrub. I tried to pull myself back to the path. I slithered, almost fell, recovered. I was up to my knees in frigid black porridge. My boots glugged and choked in peaty gunk. The branch crucified my hand. I hung on, feeling blood seep down my wrist.

"Edgar! What can I...?"

"Careful. Don't, well, maybe..."

Sylvia bent to help, struggling to keep her balance. I still held the branch, reached my right hand toward her. She grasped it, began to lean back and pull.

A haze of midges descended. Without thinking, Sylvia flailed with her free hand. Another bad mistake.

"No!" In unison.

She lost her balance, slipped. Still clutching my hand, she slid-swung past me like a gate on greased hinges and splashed into the loch. The torque twisted me, tried to yank me out there too. But I stayed put. Held on to Sylvia's hand. Held on to the thorn bush. My bleeding fingers clenched the branch with fear-fueled strength.

Sylvia, facing sideways, was in the water almost up to her waist. She turned her head to me. Distress made her beautiful. Her eyes were wide. I could see the white, indifferent moon in her pupils. She tried to pivot her body. Couldn't. Tried to lean over to add her free hand to our little love knot. It didn't work. She was trapped like a quicksand victim.

"Edgar, can you help? It's goddamn freezing. My legs are getting numb."

"Don't move. It's a steep cliff. It could drop right behind you. Let me think."

Shivering, we teeter-tottered in a bizarre yoga pose, Sylvia and the bush wrenching the ends, me as the fulcrum, arms straining out, a scarecrow.

The bagpipes wailed. Midges and sweat blurred my vision. I tasted sour blood. The water stank.

I shifted my weight. The mud tugged, treacherous, opportunistic. Sylvia's hand tried to slip through mine. She gasped. I squeezed tighter. I thought of Hitchcock's saboteur, hanging by a literal thread from top of the Statue of Liberty.

I tried to rotate my hand, tried to reshape my grip.

"No! Don't! Edgar, please! Can you...? What if you..?

"Hold still. I need to figure it out." The bagpipes stopped. Time to pay the piper.

A dark presence. In the water. In my mind. Which, both, I wasn't sure.

The stubborn ostinato of my thoughts refused to stop. Our marriage. Failing. My music. Failing. So easy to let go. One hand. Both. My pulse thudded, drumming, drumming.

The peace of twilight had become a tumult, nightfall at the loch black eddies of doubt.

"Edgar..."

"Please, Sylvia, give me a moment to think."

Road Work

Dez had been given the finger twice this morning, though his shift was barely under way.

By now he was used to getting the finger. Used to assholes like the Lexus jerk and his vicious backspray of gravel. Used to idiots like the cell-phoning bitch with her scary one-handed turn. Used to fuming, red-faced pricks slewing into abrupt 180s.

Take it out on the flagman.

Rude and angry drivers were getting to be the norm. Well, fuck 'em. Who were they to look down on him?

Remington said to write such people up, but how the hell do you read license plates when you're dodging rocks or diving aside? How do you remember numbers when your blood pressure's demanding a coronary?

"Get their number and we'll do a number on them," said Remington, who loved inventing turns of phrase. As bosses went, Remington was OK. For one thing, he was adamant about making sure relief arrived on time. "There's nothing badder than an anxious bladder," he'd say. Dez couldn't agree more.

In his former job—his 'real' job, as he thought of it—junior execs had their own washroom, separate from the plebes. Dez had risen to that gratifying perk just months before the layoff slaughter. Now he had access to a stifling portacan in the boonies.

Despite the big comedown, despite the lurching redirection in his life, Dez at least had a job. He knew he was lucky. Most of his traumatized colleagues were still hungry.

On Bloodbath Friday, Dez was smart enough not to waste time handwringing and whining. While others cried their way to neighborhood bars, Dez grit his teeth and drove to the unemployment office, filled out forms. A sagging bulletin board advised of a flagger certification course. Dez plunged in, passed, snagged an opening, and here he was, stopgap. Stopgap with a stop sign.

He'd traded his silk-blend suits and hand-painted ties for an angry red hardhat, a smoldering orange vest and what Remington called combat boots. "Out here, we make war, not love."

Dez answered a question from a peeved SUV driver, resisted the urge to punch him out, and returned to his reverie. One thing about this job was that it let him think, almost meditate. There never was time for that in the corporate madhouse. Here, between bursts of traffic, he could contemplate at length.

This morning, he fretted about rent and support payments. Everything was really tight. He worried about his daughter. Annie was suffering. How do you deal with divorce at age six? His ex wasn't helping much, engrossed with her new boyfriend. Dez had taken his vows seriously, assumed a lifelong partnership, and whoa! Knocked off course just seven years in. Blindsided. When he thought of Jen cheating with that sleazeball lawyer, his chest constricted.

A convoy of vehicles appeared. His radio crackled.

"Got a pause. Keep 'em coming, big boy." That was Madge, up the road. Single mother, chubby, flirtatious.

Road Work

He sent the cars, trying not to return driver scowls. "Last one's the blue Fusion," he said into his radio. Madge acknowledged cheerfully. "Attaway, McGuire!"

Dez wondered if there was such a thing as walkie-talkie sex. He hadn't made love in so long, even FM hanky-panky might be pretty good. On the other hand, why encourage Madge? Their only common ground was being down on their luck, stuck here flagging.

How the fuck can she still smile so much?

The air stank of diesel. The sun scorched. A pickup horn savaged his eardrums. Insect bites irritated his face. Sweat and grime chafed his neck. His left foot throbbed. His right hip ached. This was not why he'd earned an MBA.

Up rolled his relief in a battle-scarred minivan. "Ready to go smoke a joint, Desmond?" Porky leaned out the window and coughed a laugh. "Your fairy godfather's here." Porky's face looked like the desert floor after a gullywasher. He was the skinniest person Dez had ever seen. A lifer.

A lifer flagman. *Is this where I'm heading? Shit.*

Dez took a merciful pee in the portajohn, yanked off his oppressive hardhat, slouched in his Chevy beater, wondered who got his BMW. He nibbled a power bar fortified with dust and checked the cellphone he could barely afford.

No messages. Employers ignored him. How many resumes out? He'd lost count.

He wanted to call Annie, but she'd be in school. Were they teaching her about real life? Why spoil what innocence remained after she'd watched her parents battle? Forget 'Stop, Drop and Roll'. It's 'Fight, Scream and Split'.

Follow your dreams, and life rewards you with a stop sign.

During his time off, when he wasn't trying to reassure Annie or squabbling with Jen, Dez searched for jobs, reworked resumes, rewrote cover letters. Nothing. There was more action in the sour sludge in his thermos.

Sun ablaze, the days dragged on. Construction vehicles creaked, clattered and roared. Traffic sputtered, complained. Drivers glared, checked their watches. Dez stood at his station, sweated, rotated his pole. Slow. Stop. Slow. Stop. For companions he had grit, bugs and exhaust fumes.

And he had his thoughts. They were often negative, frequently morose. But he felt something useful trying to rise.

He remembered flagger safety training. He wondered if he could have been more alert in his prior life. Never turn your back. Always have an escape route. Don't be fearful, but allow for possibilities. *Including change.*

Monday, he zoned out behind sunglasses, pondering betrayal and illusions. A broken backhoe, traffic trapped, engines off. Flies buzzed, settled.

Some instinct made him stare inside a shiny black Caddy. Its owner, a silver-haired CEO type, had been apoplectic when forced to stop. He'd yammered heatedly at his cell.

Now something seemed wrong about his silhouette.

Dez strode to the car, saw the slumped figure, yanked open the door. The guy sagged. Ashen blue face. No apparent breathing.

Dez grabbed the walkie-talkie.

"This is Dez. Call 911, get an ambulance. Driver heart attack. And send another flagger."

He released the shoulder harness, slid the man to the ground and began CPR as best he could remember it. He kept the sequence going until the EMTs took over.

After the ambulance sirened off, it was back to the job, his own heart racing the rest of the day.

Weeks later, grudging thanks from the man, recovering. A certificate of achievement, unframed. An official handshake, clammy.

What Dez mostly recalled of the incident, he realized with amusement, was that he'd worried about getting mud on the $900 suit.

Dez began to develop an ironic inner voice, found he could again laugh at himself. He rediscovered his sense of humor. He joshed with Remington, teased Madge on the two-way, and enjoyed real laughs with Porky, who turned out to be an interesting character, not only a genius at sneaky on-the-job smoking but a master of the fretless guitar, happy with his job, and very much in charge of his life. Not a loser at all.

Talk about misreading a guy. *I'm a snob,* Dez realized. *A fucking snob.*

He began to understand that flagging gave him authority. He felt more in command than he'd ever been. Traffic stopped when he raised his hand. Moved when he turned his paddle. Despite driver ire and disdain, he was boss. Even cop cars had to pay him mind, sitting there idling, docile, panting, tongues out, waiting for their master's favorable signal. The boss.

"I've been watching you, McGuire." Remington handed Dez his pay packet. The trailer reeked of creosote. "You gotta smile more. A smile goes a mile." He held up his hand.

"But aside from that, you got something. You're hitting a rhythm out there. You got grace, man. Keep it up."

Grace. Not a word Dez connected with himself. But it was there, in more ways than one.

He'd developed almost-balletic moves when he turned his paddle. Pivoted like a matador and twirled the pole with flair. Ole! Instead of the finger, drivers gave him the thumbs up.

"You're a class act, Dez," said Madge, going off-shift. She'd brought by some homemade fudge. No flirtation. Genuine feeling. The fudge tasted great.

Dez started enjoying his work. He defused disgruntled drivers with poise and humor. He smiled at bad weather, kept stray dogs safe, gracefully adapted to revised procedures and difficult locations.

He took command of his thoughts, directing them like traffic. He brainstormed ideas for opening a business, ideas for retraining. And, most important, ideas for working amicably with Jen to help Annie feel loved and secure.

Road Work

He knew he wouldn't be a flagman forever—though that notion no longer seemed nightmarish—and he loved being able to leave his work at work, his eighty dollar neckties in the closet.

Life wasn't easier. It was just different. Change wasn't his enemy. He could deal with it. He thought often of a maxim from good old Remington.

"You'll really swing once you learn you're king. King of your road."

Shades of Gray

Gemma saw something in the mist, wraiths drifting amid graygreen splotches of foliage—tendrils of fog or fur, she couldn't quite tell which. She raised her binoculars. Focus, dammit, focus! God yes, a wolf—focus!—no, two wolves. One gray, one a soft charcoal. Waiting. If they sensed her, they didn't show it. Or didn't care. Long tongues out, lapping the morning air. Sharp eyes. Cunning, Gemma thought. These could be the ones who got poor old Marrock, her favorite ram. *Goddammit, from now on, the rifle comes with me.*

A male and a female. A bonded pair, she thought, feeling a momentary stab of what—envy? Loss. Grief. Those for sure. *Mack, oh Mack.* Gemma's eyes teared, the mist drifted, the wolves vanished.

Weeping, she leaned against a rough, unsympathetic pine. Mack's sudden death left her with a multitude of worries. About being alone. About keeping things going. About the mortgage, paying the hired men, the vet's bills, putting in hay for winter. About her son's detachment, her daughter's future. And now she had these predators gnawing at her mind.

Gnawing? The word made her laugh through her tears, then she cried afresh, thinking of Marrock's savaged carcass sprawled in the bloodied earth.

Anger flared, and Gemma pushed away from the tree. She would take these wolves just like Mack would have done.

Mack. I take thee, Donald McLaren Larch, to be mine. And you were my everything for well over forty years.

They met on the blustery UW campus when they dashed into a doorway to get out of the rain. History and engineering colliding, love at first drenching. They were married soon after they graduated. On another rainy day.

After working only eight or nine months, Mack decided he didn't want to be an engineer. He convinced Gemma that they should move to Idaho, promising they could always leave if she asked, something she never did. With a small inheritance, they bought some land and some livestock, and here they'd been ever since, Ketch born two years after they'd moved, Roxanne much later, surprising Mack and Gemma long after they'd settled into their ranching routine.

Gemma walked back to her horse and rode down from the woods, already thinking about how to track and kill the wolves. As she descended the slope, she gazed at the distant mountains. The Pioneers always held her in thrall. The unseasonable fog added an extra sense of mystery.

Mack died of a huge heart attack while they were out mending fences. Gemma had turned to look at the Pioneers, relishing a moment of deep pleasure. One minute Mack was behind her, energetically working the post hole digger, the one she'd painted a wild neon pink so they'd find it anywhere, and the next minute he was on the ground, gone.

In the months since Mack's death, Gemma had been attempting to run the sheep ranch herself. She had part-time help from Alberto and Jorge, two Peruvian guys, and she counted on Roxy's eventual return for moral support and companionship. Gemma even held a faint hope that Ketch, the prodigal son, might come back some day.

Life here was all about stubbornness. Gemma knew she was as stubborn as the most recalcitrant of her sheep. As stubborn as the deep-set boulders infesting the landscape. As stubborn as the cheat grass, blown in from elsewhere to sink extensive, tenacious roots. Hell, as stubborn as Mack himself, insisting they leave Seattle to settle in this outback.

As Gemma rode toward the ranch house, she glanced toward the edge of the foothills. Her ever-busy sheep were little white patches against the green and brown. Somewhere up there, Alberto and the two canny old collies, Skye and Trick, would be keeping watch. Suddenly, a phrase of Bach ran through her head. "*Sheep may safely graze...*" Mack loved to sing that in his hearty tenor. She stopped to dab her eyes with her bandana.

Gemma put the horse in the corral and crossed to the house. The kitchen reeked of magic markers. Roxy, wearing one of her mother's faded denim shirts, sat at the kitchen table, coloring flow charts. She was home on term break from Washington State. Soon she would graduate, then it was into veterinary studies. After that, Gemma prayed, Roxy would work close by, maybe no further than Hailey. Or even move home and make the ranch her base.

Gemma poured some coffee. "Wolves," she announced, plunking down across from her daughter. "Two of them. Another headache to deal with."

Roxy closed her laptop. "Mom" was all she needed to say.

"I know, I know," said Gemma, sipping. "You ecology types are all alike, but fact is I gotta shoot them. These two are making us their territory. Next thing, a whole pack'll be down here."

"No, fact is you don't have to shoot them, Mom." Roxy pushed back some strands of red hair. "Preemptive strikes are Pentagon tactics. They're not appropriate here. Let the wolves be."

They'd had this discussion before, in one form or another. Gemma loved seeing Roxy flex her growing intellect and developing moral sense, even if the two of them sometimes didn't agree.

Roxy clearly enjoyed their talks, something Ketch had rarely seemed to do. Ketch flared up easily. Especially with Mack. Resentment. Angry retorts. Defensiveness. After the big blowup—the one with a capital B—Ketch had boarded a bus to California before his parents knew what hit them. He hadn't returned, except—grudgingly it seemed—for Mack's funeral, where he was thinner, blonder and more distant than ever. To say they were estranged was an overstatement, but it was hard to imagine Ketch ever moving back. Sheep ranching was not the life for him. Neither were small Idaho communities and their conservative values.

Roxy for sure had all the right stuff. Brains, sensitivity, a love of the wild, a strong artistic side. When it came to drawing birds, she could out-Audubon old J. J. himself. When it came to defending wildlife, she toted a big soapbox.

"Humans are always tilting ecosystems out of balance," Roxy was saying. "Protect the sheep if you have to. Get a Great Pyrenees. Put a donkey out there, for God's sake. But don't shoot any wolves, Mom. Don't."

Gemma held her tongue. She could have reminded Roxy of Esk, their Great Pyrenees of about fifteen years ago, pursuing a lone wolf and fatally ambushed by a waiting pack. She also knew about guard donkeys but couldn't afford one, let alone the time for it to bond with the sheep.

"Well, I'll think about it," she said. "But if those wolves keep hanging around, I've gotta take action. I'm sorry, but there it is."

On her rounds Gemma began taking her classic Winchester fitted with Mack's favorite scope, a big old Bushnell. He'd taught her how to use both, *and it's a good thing,* she thought. *"I'm ready, Mack."* She was vigilant, but by the end of the week the wolves hadn't reappeared.

As the day for returning to Pullman grew close, Roxy seemed withdrawn. Gemma put it down to the barrage of term papers. But at supper on the final night, Roxy shoved aside her uneaten pie, looked her mother in the eye, and said, very calmly, "Mom, I need to tell you a couple of things."

"If it's about the wolves..." Gemma started.

"No, it's about me. The thing is Mom, I'm pregnant," Roxy said, holding up her hand to forestall interruption. "And I'm pretty sure I'll get an abortion."

"Wait, wait. Abortion? What?" Gemma rounded the table and crouched before her daughter, taking her hands. "Pregnant? Roxy, how're you feeling?"

"I'm OK. Look, I've thought it through. Maybe I'll have kids someday, but now is not the right time."

"Are you asking for my blessing for an abortion? Is that it? I can't. It's your decision, but I can't..." Tears filled Gemma's eyes.

"I've always valued your opinion, Mom," said Roxy gently. "A lot. But I have to decide this on my own."

"Then why are you telling me?" Gemma asked, with a touch of bitterness. "I needn't have known."

"I don't want secrets between us, Mom."

Gemma squeezed Roxy's hands. "Are you a hundred percent sure? I mean about an abortion."

"God, no! It's been tormenting me all week. But it's way too early in my life to have a kid. And, well..." Roxy shrugged.

Gemma made a face. "You don't need me spouting pro-life clichés. I'm personally against abortion. But I'll admit I'm selfish too. You know how much I want grandchildren. And Ketch sure isn't going to provide any."

Roxy gave a wry smile. "I suppose not. But you're going to have to wait. I need to finish school, and then there's so much I want to do before I have babies."

Gemma couldn't help herself. "But college students have babies! Vets have babies! Besides, you know I'd help you raise him. Her."

They talked and talked, Gemma making a fresh pot of coffee, and Roxy, suddenly very hungry, devouring the rest of the pie.

It was all give and take, but no real budging. At one point, Gemma, in exasperation, blurted out it was odd that Roxy wanted to protect the wolves but not a new human life.

"You gotta be kidding, Mom! It's not odd. They're two vastly different issues. But why not flip that idea around? You want to save a tiny fetus but are ready to kill two full-grown, intelligent animals. Is that consistent?"

Gemma thought about it. "All right. What if we trade? You keep the baby and I don't shoot the wolves."

"Mom." As usual, that one word said everything.

"When did life get so complex?"

Roxy grimaced. "Well, I hope my other news doesn't make it even more complex. See, Mom, there's a change in plans. I'll finish my degree, but I'm not going to vet school. Not now anyway. Maybe never."

"What?" Gemma was stunned.

"After I graduation I'm moving to New York City. I want to see if I can make it as an artist. Study, draw, paint, immerse myself. Another reason a baby wouldn't fit into things."

Gemma flopped back in her chair. "It feels like you've just fired both barrels at me, sweetheart."

"I didn't mean to pile it on at once. I couldn't work up the courage to tell you earlier or in stages. I'm sorry."

Gemma looked at the large wall photo of Mack shearing a sheep. Mack was grinning. The ewe wasn't. "I wonder what your Dad would have thought of all this."

"Dad always said to follow my dreams."

"But the ranch. I always hoped. Well, at least that you'd be near by."

"I probably will—one day. But not right now." Roxy hugged her mother. "And Mom, you always said to listen to my heart. I couldn't have had better advice—from either of you."

"Jeez, Roxy, you really know how to add novelty to an old gal's life, don't you?"

At last they went to bed, still pondering uncertainties. Gemma's list of worries had grown. So much seemed to be about loss. Mack, gone forever. An unborn grandchild, maybe about to perish. Ketch, staying away in San Francisco. Roxy, heading east. These goddam wolves wanting the sheep.

As she fell fitfully to sleep, Gemma kept fretting about the wolves. Maybe at least they were something she could directly tackle. As if on cue, a wolf howled in the distance. Or did she imagine it?

Early the next morning, filled with doubts, each made a promise to think about things. Roxy's little Honda rolled off, flicking gravel at the lower pasture fence. Gemma waved with a false heartiness.

Sunup. Lots to be done.

Shades of Gray

As she finished saddling her horse, she noticed a hawk circling lazily over one of her fields. Beyond it, a shift in the clouds sent a slow sweep of sidelight across the distant hills, illuminating hidden contours and ridges. *That's what insight must be like*, she thought. *Something suddenly seen from a different angle or in a different light.* But she had no insights about any of her worries. No insights about Roxy's pregnancy.

"I don't want secrets between us," Roxy had said. *Oh, sweetheart, there are always secrets.* Why didn't she tell Roxy the big one? Early on, Mack and Gemma vowed Roxy should never know how close they came to aborting her because of Gemma's health. What would Roxy do if she learned about that now? Would it make a difference? For sure, telling her would throw even more chaos into her thinking.

The clouds moved on, the light changed, and the hills resumed their morning contemplations. Gemma started her rounds.

In her nervous humming, Bach had given way to bits of "Peter and the Wolf." *Dum dum dadum dum dum.* As a girl, she'd loved that story. Come to think of it, so had Ketch and Roxy, growing up. No complaints back then about shooting wolves. *That's what comes of teaching kids to think for themselves.*

Gemma finished consulting with Jorge about a lame ewe. The fear-frozen creature, released, wiggled its plump wooly rump in a crazy hopscotch of escape. Riding slowly down the slope, Gemma was still smiling. She loved her sheep, and she'd named many of them. *Glory. Jezebel. Curly. Marrock.*

The image of her dead ram galled her. She reined in her horse, thought a moment, then rode west to the area where she'd last seen the wolves. She doubted they'd return to the same place, but perhaps it was worth another look.

She crept quietly into the woods, now and then stopping to use her binoculars. Sweat slalomed down her cheek. A fly droned by. Somewhere a bird chattered angrily.

At the back edge of the woods, she noticed a gentle ripple in the pale grass. Two soft shapes swayed in and out of the fronds, a sensual dance. Slowing her breathing, Gemma tracked them with the binoculars. Gray. Charcoal. The same pair. She felt another tug of envy at their togetherness. What are they doing? Had their den been here all the time? It had to be. The female was pregnant, teats beginning to swell. Dammit!

What will Roxy do about the abortion? What should I do? Where's Mack when you need him?

Gemma put the crosshairs on the female, changed to the male, aimed away at a hemlock, back again to the bigger wolf. He raised his head slightly, his yellow eyes beautiful and menacing. Her finger tightened on the trigger. She thought of herself as decisive. But now her mind was gyrating. The rifle wavered. *Male? Female? Warning?*

Thou shalt not kill. Kill the wolves but spare the child. Kill the child but spare the wolves. What will Roxy do? What should I do?

Gemma blinked, took a breath, squeezed the trigger.

Long Road Home

Nothing is what it seems.

In Iraq you learn that quickly or you could be very very dead very very fast.

It's all mirages.

In the desert, heat and dust and sweat make blurry illusions out of upended trucks, a crumbled wall, a waving kid. Any trust you might have had turns tail and flees the first time that kid morphs into a ragged, raging imam erupting with fire which rips your buddies into wet confetti.

One misstep, you lose a leg, your pecker, for sure your sanity if not your life. One going close to a toothy smile wrapped in a bomb and at last you learn for sure if there's a heaven or a hell. Or a nothing.

The barometric pressure and the pulsing fear pound your eyeballs and your skull with a thumping you can't lose even in your dreams. You're drenched with terror. It never washes off.

I guess some of us are lucky. So now I'm going home. The first time in 16 months, three days, two hours and 25 minutes. Every tension-filled second marked off in my journal. Yeah, I keep a journal as a way to talk to my sweetheart, my family, my once-normal self. I wear it beneath my combat gear, close to my heart. Last resort against shrapnel. Against craziness.

Now this lumbering bus, bizarrely ordinary on a tree-speckled North Carolina road.

Old ladies in broadbrim hats, wicker shopping baskets perched primly above. In Tikrit those baskets would have been shredded by precautionary fire at 50 meters.

Bunch of teens giggling through some talky word game. Lord, they tattoo early these days, but nothing like the tatts you see over there. 24/7 on the edge brings out the grim imagination, the ghoulish art.

Fat couple squeezed sloppily into their seats. They make Americans big these days, up a size or more from when I left. At least they look happy, murmuring together. And those drips on the back of his neck are pure southern summer sweat, not anxiety, not horror, not blood.

Dozing guy in rumpled overalls and dusty boots, string-tied package in his lap—in Basra we'd have our eyes tight on him from the getgo.

Up there, the driver, balding head bobbing a bit to an inner song, shortsleeved arms coaxing the big wheel into a curve, uniform jacket swinging in time on the back of his seat. No steel pot, no vest, no goggles, no armor plate, no reading the advancing terrain with high adrenalin. Just a good old boy rolling his one-horse convoy down a country lane.

And me. I wonder if they've got me pegged even in this faded tee and jeans. I've got the look, but then again maybe there's still innocence abroad. Maybe reality doesn't leach down to these back towns and hills. Maybe I'm just a guy out for a bus ride.

One of the teens claps his hands. The prettiest girl laughs. That's a sound you miss over there, girlish

Long Road Home

laughter, though it would be buried, chopped to nothing under the small arms clatter the shells whooping the yelling the screaming the wailing. And always that thumping.

I used to know true laughter, not just the nervous, wet-your-pants kind that follows knowing you're still alive when hell has raged past. I used to know silence. The reassuring song of bees. The insolence of crickets. The lazy plop of mountain ash berries kissing the undergrowth. I used to know silence and gentleness and the day turning slowly toward evening, the twinkling fireflies and stars in peaceful competition. God, am I coming back to that or dragging the whole nightmare with me to taint, distort, obliterate?

Does this bumping bus ride home feel good? I guess it should. Too bad relief never hits you as fast as shock, contentment never latches on with the speed of dread.

A small lurch, a grinding of gears. I reach for my M-4 but find only my floppy backpack sprawled on the seat beside me. My hands clasp urgently at it anyway, wanting.

The bus is slowing, and ahead we can see a figure by the side of the road, one arm held out like a signpost, a sort of salute.

We're on one of those rare old-fashioned whistlestop, flag-it-down routes. Some guy, a farmhand, a motorist with a breakdown, a tired hiker, wants a ride. So why is my heart racing? Why do my eyes ache? Breathe, I tell myself. Breathe slowly. Slower. Watch.

The bus whines to a stop, brakes hissing softly. The driver scratches his head with one hand and reaches out with the other to lever open the door. Warm, sweet huckleberry air swirls in. Someone clumps up the steps. A tall, wiry man, early 60's, roughshaven, baggy dark shirt, fatigue pants. Nervously, he drags up an old, stained army duffel bag and leans it heavily under the windshield.

All eyes are on this diversion, this unexpected pause in the journey. Even the teens stop their game to see what novelty might be coming aboard. My heart roars, my eyes have narrowed, my hearing is on full alert, my nose strains, sniffing for cordite or blood or death.

A mumbled exchange, money fumbled for and handed over. The driver, now official, insists on tearing and punching a ticket from his pad.

Suddenly the newcomer curses at his duffel, reaches into it, yelling something like 'no, no no!' which to me is 'go, go go' and I'm sprinting down the aisle with an ancient scream of attack, stumbling over an outstretched leg, falling forward, knowing I have only seconds to neutralize this sick bastard who wide-eyed and twitching has pulled something round from the duffel as I hit him low and hard and we smash sideways down the steps and tumble out onto the roadside weeds.

I'm on top and have trapped his arms behind him with my knees and I'm ready to break his neck when the battered army canteen rolls off the bus and thunks wetly down beside us, dripping apple juice.

I turn the guy over and peer into his panting wildness, stare deep into a mirror of my own darkness.

"Viet Nam," he whimpers.

Maestro

Petrie was conducting the Bellevue Philharmonic, taking the 'Jupiter' finale at a ferocious pace. "Forget *molto allegro*," he'd joked. "I want *molten allegro*."

A stud rebelled. In the middle of the inverse quintuple counterpoint, it sprang free. Leapt from Petrie's shirt. Launched itself toward the cellos. A black pearl hurtling into space. Mozart would have giggled.

Petrie followed the stud to its apogee, traced its descent. It landed near the feet of Helen Kerr. She didn't notice. Her thighs clenched her cello. Fiercely.

Irony on irony. The studs were a gift from Petrie's wife Alex, mementos of their diving adventures in Tahiti. But it was Helen's legs he most remembered wrapping tightly around him as he dove into her. Often. Until a month ago, when Helen learned about the timpanist. "Her? You're banging a percussionist?" Helen said, witty even in distress. *Sic transit amor*. At the moment Helen appeared oblivious to anything but the raptures of Mozart.

Too bad the affair was over. Too bad the Bellevue Phil might soon drop to a tidy paragraph on his resume. Petrie was gunning for more. A lot more. He'd been noticed, and the next step, with any luck, was San Francisco.

The upstart Bellevue Philharmonic was giving the venerable Seattle Symphony a run for its money. The principal reason: Jamison Petrie. His smart programming, unorthodox interpretations, impeccable showmanship, upper crust English charm and Hugh Grant looks had brought rapid growth to the fledgling orchestra. Audiences stomached the impossible traffic across Lake Washington to watch him conduct. They queued in the rain for his concerts, soaked in anticipation. They endured the buckling, musty seats of the old movie theater to gasp at his dramatic downbeats. They crushed each other in the stage door alley. Ignored the rancid stench of overfull dumpsters and the angry crunch of broken glass. Waved sweaty programs, pleading for autographs. Classical music fans became classical music fanatics. They loved Jamison Petrie.

Shaking back his unruly hair, he plunged the symphony into the coda and rode the joyous adrenalin to the end.

The instant he lowered his arms—echoing a fluid gesture he'd seen in 'Swan Lake'—the audience pegged the applause meter. Feet thumped, seats clunked. *Not yet.* Petrie smiled at his musicians. The horns shook out spit. The concertmaster dabbed his brow. Helen gazed into space.

He remained facing away from the audience. Whistles, cheers. *Plebian, but I'll take it.* Eventually, he gave another balletic sweep. The orchestra rose. The applause intensified. *Right.* And at last he turned, slowly, to accept the light, the warmth, the love. He felt very much like Jupiter—planet or God—on top of it all. *As good as sex, maybe better.*

Maestro

"Is this yours, Mr. Petrie?" One of the second cellos stood nervously in the doorway of Petrie's dressing room. He held out the stud.

Petrie accepted the pearl. It wobbled like a roulette ball in his palm. "Thanks very much." The cellist turned to leave. Petrie searched for the man's name. "Close the door behind you, would you, Victor? Cheers."

The door shut with a satisfying click. Petrie wrenched off his black tie and shrugged off his dark jacket. The sweating began in earnest. It intrigued him that often his body avoided perspiring until the music had ended and then released it all at once.

"Well, that's got 'er, then, mate," he said to his ancient teddy bear. Dabby leaned indolently against the table mirror, his ginger fur shocked and spiked. Petrie's wife was responsible for Dabby's look. Alex hated Dabby's slight gasworks odor. Early in the marriage, she ordered their housekeeper to put the bear in the laundry. The washing only intensified the smell. And it gave Dabby his wild eccentricity.

Dabby had been with Petrie for 41 years. The bear attended every rehearsal, every concert. Good luck talisman, confidant, cheerleader. The child which Petrie didn't have. Not the same as flesh and blood, but essential. He was one of Petrie's two most beloved possessions. The other was a first edition score of Beethoven's Fifth Symphony. Whenever Petrie looked at the yellowed pages, he felt reverent, almost giddy. Not the same as owning something in the master's hand, but close.

Petrie thought of Beethoven now. San Francisco wanted the Third Symphony as part of the audition, and already Petrie was toying with new approaches. *Knock their knickers off.*

He took a long drink of scrumpy. He imported his favorite cider from Derbyshire. Raising the glass, he toasted the bear. "Right. I'm away soon, lad. Bit o' scuba dooba, an' then it's fookin' Frisco right enough." Few besides Dabby ever heard the Midlands accent. Petrie preferred to present upper class refinement, just a hint of the BBC.

He stripped off his shirt, toweled vigorously. Slipped on a clean shirt. Checked himself in the mirror. Blinked. A small boy looked shyly back, blue eyes pleading. Petrie blinked again, erased the vision. He straightened his collar. Slowly walked out into the dark corridor. Paused. Breathed deeply. Strode toward the enthusiastic hum washing toward him from the green room.

Three days later, Petrie sank into the amniotic embrace of the Caribbean. He was diving off the island of Roatan. Perfect water temperature, surreal clarity. He hovered near the wall at thirty feet, disregarding the group, which was further down. His assigned buddy, feeling ignored, had teamed up with the dive master, and Petrie was free to enjoy the solitude. He listened to the intermittent bubbles, the crunching of parrot fish nibbling coral, the hollow vibrations from a boat engine, a ground bass.

He floated closer to the wall to watch seahorses, green and grey grace notes hanging on strands of grass.

Just below him, ferns of soft coral swayed in a complex tempo di ballo: pinks, yellows, blacks, browns. Some turned red as undulating shafts of light caressed them.

He turned to swim slowly after a lion fish. Medieval and majestic. *A fellow with flair,* Petrie thought. All spines, feathery fins and wild antennas, red and black. He remembered hearing this was an intruder in Honduran waters. The fish belonged in the Pacific.

The creature eyed Petrie through craggy slits, a primal gaze, dismissed him, imperious. *A fine conductor candidate. Panache. Opportunistic. Predatory. Survival of the...*

A shadow crossed over him. He shivered, looked up. Just above, indifferent to his presence, swam a spotted eagle ray. The dark wings moved with languid grace. Conducting a luxuriously slow waltz. Petrie turned and followed, blissful.

Suddenly Petrie became aware the current had changed. He had drifted away from the safe zone of the dive site. He kicked firmly, found himself still pulled against his will. He realized the rest of the dive group must have moved in near the end of the wall, close to the tip of the island. He was out here, about to be tugged off toward Belize. Even as he struggled and his brain rushed through choices, his mind was sardonic. *"Conductor's body found on Yucatan beach."*

Panic seeped into his consciousness. Petrie hadn't truly panicked since the days his parents had yanked him from familiar Derbyshire boyhood streets, flown him thousands of miles and plunked him down in a New

England mill town. And even then his panic eventually gave way to a resilience found in new friends and in new experiences. A resilience found in the sounds of factory whistles, songbirds, a beggar's hurdy-gurdy. A resilience strengthened by discovering he had musical talent, a way to claim an identity.

But now, as he fought the grasp of the current, panic began asserting itself. His pulse thumped, an insane percussionist. His breathing shot into accelerando. His muscles screamed a dissonant chorus of complaints.

Struggling, he heard something else arise in his head. Timed to his leaping heart rate, up flew fragments from *Scheherazade* and the nurse's darting motif from *Romeo and Juliet* and then, startlingly, the fugue from his own suite, *Puget Soundings*. All trying to deflect his anxiety. From underneath rose the refrains of his old Filipino dive master. He heard Bayani's singsong voice crooning a litany of wisdom. Petrie grasped frantically at a counter-intuitive idea. Instead of going up, he took himself deeper. *Into a lower register.* The current seemed a tiny bit slower. *So to the bass.* He went lower still, and yet lower. *Off the ledger lines into the unreadable music, the unreadable depths.* What did his gauge show? Didn't matter; it either worked or...

It worked. He reached a point below the main current.

Orienting himself, staying deep, he slowly swam back toward the west shore. A distant ship's engine grumbled, a mordant bassoon, chastening.

"I doubt you were really in any trouble, Jamie." Alex tick-tocked in the woven hammock, a rare moment of slowing down.

Petrie gulped his rum punch. *Why did I bother telling her?* His wife forever seemed to challenge death, spitting at the fate which killed her parents in a plane crash when she was seven.

Alex had agreed to join him briefly on Roatan before flying to a shoot in Costa Rica. She sipped her pina colada. "Besides, we know that boyish magic of yours can charm the pants off anything. Even the ocean."

Petrie grunted. Inwardly he shuddered, remembering the feel of terror, the absence of control. Alex didn't get it. Why should she? She thought of them both as infallible. Steadying a shaking hand, he held his glass up to the sunset, admiring the gold of the punch, the deepening redgold beyond. He took a long breath. A piece of ice clinked. An acceptable B flat. Two dolphins arched silver across the glittering waters between the palm-strewn keys.

Alexandra LeClaire was a shark. Internationally-known, traveling constantly for her photography, she devoured the world. She devoured people, especially men.

They'd met on a beach in Kenya. He was diving in the Indian Ocean after a guest-conducting stint in London. She had just finished a photo study of the Maasai. He was euphoric, having seen his first whale shark. She was elated over the growing success of her 'Faces of the Earth' series. They fascinated each other.

Circled. Warily. They were aroused less by sex than by the friction of competitive creative wills.

Five years of marriage hadn't changed anything. Alex was sexually voracious, perhaps more than Jamie. She seemed indifferent to his philandering. She found it useful as a springboard for her own fantasies. He thought she'd been especially frisky these two nights on Roatan. *Who's on her mind?*

Ants had discovered the ceiling of the resort bedroom. The made a thin black stuttering trail above the bed.

"So who's the lucky one this month?" Alex whispered, stroking the soft down of Jamie's back. "Still that blonde who says 'hit me!' all the time? The drummer?"

"Percussionist. Aye, she's around. Still into hitting. But a fortnight ago I fell in love."

Alex shoved him aside. "That's not allowed, dammit." The ants stopped moving.

He pulled her to him again. "Wait to hear the story, 'lex. Everything's tickety-boo. You know what a blind audition is?"

She nodded. The ants resumed their trek.

"Right. So we're auditioning violinists, sight unseen, no names, just numbers. I'm making notes behind the screen. Heard a few good fiddlers. Then number eleven starts to play. The sound is so extraordinary and so seductive, I can hardly stand it. It's Hilary Hahn in heaven, Anne Sophie Mutter on ambrosia. A tone as pure as I've ever heard, technique to make Perlman chuck in his bow. How could I not fall in love? Don't get restless, pet. So I'm turned on—in every department—and hot and eager to meet number eleven. Well, bollocks! It turns out to be a guy. With a goatee. And bad breath." Jamie laughed. "But it almost made no difference to me, his music was so incredible. I had fallen in love."

Alex rolled over on top of him. "Jamie, you could fall in love with anyone. Anything. You could fall in love with an octopus."

"I have," he said. "More than once."

"Well," she said, pressing against him. "Now I'll tell you about my beautiful French journalist, and the crooked little scar on his prick. Looked exactly like... Um, speaking of which, where are the condoms?"

"What?"

"Condoms. Dr. McGowan doesn't want me back on the pill."

"Why do we need anything? C'mon, Alex."

"Get a damn condom. I'm not rolling the dice. Not with you. Not with anyone."

"Isn't it about time?"

"Not that again."

He tried a grin. "With our genes we'd produce a bloody genius."

"Why keep bringing this up? Nothing's changed."

"Yeah it has. We're older. A boy. A nice little boy. Maybe twins, what do you think?"

Something light dropped on Alex's shoulder. An ant. Shuddering, Alex rolled away. She scowled.

"Isn't your stupid bear enough of a kid for you? Hold him, for fuck's sake."

Petrie was still thinking about children as he flew back to Seattle, his headsets pulsing with French chamber music. He wanted to be a father. To do it right. To relive so many things he'd missed. To feel deeply outside the world of music. He thought a lot about parenthood. His own Mum and Dad were a study in not how to do it. *Follow the rules. Keep your nose clean. Respect the bloody belt. What more is there?*

They'd been bold enough to emigrate from dirty old Belper, but crossing the Atlantic didn't improve their parenting. Or turn them into sophisticates. They remained modest, conservative people. Bert, risen from gritty foundry roots, became a pretty decent craftsman in iron. *An iron hand, aye.* Dottie parleyed a bit of education into keeping books for a small tool and die business. *By the books.* They clung to traditions. To rules. But at least they had the smarts not to interfere when their son showed surprising musical talent. When he won scholarship after scholarship, they seemed proud enough. At a distance. But in no way did they understand him. As he advanced they were indifferent to, or perhaps just ignorant of, his skills and his stature.

Only once did Bert and Dottie come to see him conduct. They trundled up to watch his guest appearance in Hartford. He was taken aback by their clothes. Over thirty years in this country and they were still wearing sturdy British tweeds. Both of them. His mother allowed a half-hug. His father granted a lukewarm handshake.

Maestro

After the concert—an easy diet of Schubert, Ravel and Copland—Petrie's parents stood uncomfortably back stage.

"Ye changed yer name, eh?" Bert wheezed as he talked. "Wee Jimmy Peters is puttin' on airs, is 'ee, then?"

"I didn't half like that Bolero thing," said Dottie, fanning herself with the program. "'Brilliant."

"Aye, but don't Jim-boy look like a bloody black stork jumpin' about tha' stage?" His father snorted. "An' such grand tail feathers, eh?"

"Makes 'im more like a swallow, those," said his mother. She fixed her son with a tired stare. "And wher'd thee find that accent, Jimmy, lad? Ever so posh now, isn't he, Bert?"

The jet cleaved the clouds and descended into the green of Seattle.

Petrie had only a week at home before he was to begin running the gauntlet in San Francisco, the fourth of the five finalists.

Dabby perched on the base of a heavy desk lamp, watching Petrie marking a pile of scores. The work became tiresome. Petrie took out his Beethoven first edition, slipped on white gloves and turned the pages. He knew he should put the score in his safe deposit box, but he liked to have it close by for good luck. San Francisco had asked him to program Beethoven's Third Symphony. Pity his treasure was the Fifth. But the Third was more than enough challenge to let him show his stuff. *Back to work, Jimmy.*

The computer beeped. He was playing online chess. His move. Petrie's opponent was Stephen Escher, a friend since their student days at Julliard. As fate would have it, Escher also was a competitor for the San Francisco position. For the last three years, he'd been conducting smaller ensembles in Florida and in Texas, and he desperately wanted to move up. "God, if I see any more cockroach crap on a score, I'll commit hara kiri with my baton."

Escher's move was unorthodox, slightly sneaky, and Petrie suspected a bigger trap a few moves ahead. He wasn't going to give the bugger the satisfaction, so he stalled, castling. A moment later Escher called on Skype.

"Goddamit, Jamie, get into battle here. Gimme a little challenge, would you?" On the screen, Stephen's face seemed plumper than ever. "I'm the fattest conductor this side of a stroke," he often said. "A lock for the Guinness Book." It seemed that now he was trying to soften things with a beard.

"More important things to do," said Petrie, holding up the Bruch First Violin Concerto, another piece requested by San Francisco.

"Oh yeah. They gave me Rachmaninoff Three with Clutterhouse to tear up the piano. He'll be OK. Who's your soloist?"

"Ramon Ortega. Heard he's good."

"He is. Think they assigned you a guy so you won't get distracted by trying to sleep with the violinist?"

Petrie made a face. "Very funny, Stephen. Have you had your turn under the microscope?"

"I'm up after you. Best for last and all that." Escher leaned toward the webcam and whispered conspiratorially. "OK, big boy. What's your opinion on the others? Geraint St Ives, f'rinstance?"

"Geraint's fine." Petrie shrugged. "If you like flamboyant without focus. I can be flamboyant too, but I know exactly what I'm doing."

"Yeah, you do, don't you?" Escher scratched his beard. "Anyway, I heard he annoyed them by dinking around with Mahler. So likely Geraint it ain't."

Petrie was rummaging for another pencil. He straightened and laughed. "If you want gossip, just call Eagle-eyes Escher."

Escher beamed. "I'm your man." His cheeks became two whole notes. "And what about Guetschow? Kurt's got hotshit pedigree."

"Yes, but too pompous for me. Pompous programming, pompous style. I'd bet he even makes love using a metronome."

"You'd know about that. I wouldn't." Escher leered. "But yep. My source says the committee thinks he's old-fashioned."

"Your source?"

"You have your pillow talk, old bean. I have my boring little email contacts." Escher licked his lips. "And then there's the luscious Dr. d'Milano. My source says the little minx played up her Italian side. The panelists loved her, especially the men."

"Well, Victoria's an eyeful, all right. I saw her conduct at Marlborough. Couldn't take my eyes off her ass. Glorious. But why she's a finalist is beyond me.

Just between us, she's not ready for the big leagues. Except maybe her derriere. That's world-class."

Escher snorted. "Jamie, Jamie."

"I've got to go, Stephen."

"Hang on! What about the last two candidates? How would you describe me?"

"A devious chess player who can read music reasonably well."

"Jeez, thanks. And yourself?"

"Actually this describes both of us: 'Arrogant bastards.'

Escher smiled. "Nature of our profession, yes? Well, have fun in San Fran. Eat lots of Rice-a-Roni. Hey, my move. Watch your queen, Jamie. She'll get you into trouble. Ciao."

"I'm pregnant." Helen wasted no time in getting to the point. She had asked Petrie to meet her at Gas Works Park. He thought perhaps she wanted to start things again. He wasn't unreceptive. He liked Helen. They were walking towards the edge of Lake Union, saying little, when she crashed the cymbals.

Petrie stared at a small, scruffy-haired boy struggling to fly a long-stringed kite. High above jerked an angry yellow and green dragon, trailing flames, tormented by the wind. A jostling cacophony of colors.

"Who's the father then?" he finally got out.

"Don't be cute. Don't be offensive. There's been no one else."

He stared across the nervous waters at the gleaming Seattle skyline. A few ambiguous clouds nudged each other just above the highest towers. "I'm sorry. I didn't mean to be rude. It's just that I'm stunned."

"Look, Jamie. I've agonized for a couple of weeks. Finally I can be matter of fact. For the moment anyway."

"Hey, I want to—"

"Let me speak." Strands of her long red hair blew across her face. She pushed them back. "I know it sounds crass. Just think of this as a courtesy call, Jamie. There's probably only one option here, but I wanted to talk to you first."

Petrie turned up his collar against the breeze. Helen kicked at a pebble.

"So. Can you suggest any way out of this, Jamie? Besides the obvious?"

The wind made them turn their faces from the lake. Petrie looked at the impotent cluster of gas processing towers, the intricate interlacing of tanks, pipes and valves. Tight and as ugly and yet as paradoxically transfixing as a twelve-tone piece. Paradox. He wanted a kid. *But not this way.*

"God, Helen."

"You're not usually so eloquent, Jamie." *Sarcasm doesn't suit her.* Gulls screeched overhead.

"You know I can't..."

She walked toward the great mound. He trotted after her, uncharacteristically brought to heel. He tasted the sourness of anxiety, apprehension. It felt as though another current was pulling him off.

"Helen, I... Would you wait a moment? Look, I don't believe in abortion."

"And you'd suggest what? That I derail my career and become a single mom?"

"It wouldn't really be derailing..."

"Jamie, shut up. It's my life. So here's the deal. Can you make me an offer?"

As they neared the mound, a small flock of gulls abruptly rose, mewling in irritation.

"What? You mean money?" He saw her immediate scorn. "Oh, you mean..."

"I could have loved you, Jamie. Maybe I do. Love you. But I guess it's a fantasy to think you'd give up whatshername, your highflying wife, for a...a cellist."

They laughed at the same time, a bitter high, a somber low, a duet worthy of Verdi. They reached the mound and became human gnomons in the midst of the huge sundial. Rocks, shells, glass and bronze formed the hours underfoot. Their shadows came together, diverged.

Petrie paced.

"If you had the...the child, I could help. Financially I mean. Nannies, au pairs. That sort of thing."

Helen sighed. "Well, as I said. Just a courtesy call."

They returned to the parking lot. Helen got into her car, put down the window, looked at him. He'd led her from the podium so often he thought she was awaiting another downbeat.

This time, his silence was her cue.

"Well, that's it then." She started the engine.

"I wish...I wish you'd..."

"Good luck in San Francisco." The car began to move off.

"Helen, I'm so sorry..." Gravel crunched. He doubted she heard him.

He thought he felt the first drops of rain. He touched his cheek. It was wet.

More than once, Petrie had watched waterspouts racing across the Coral Sea. In San Francisco, he felt he was in the midst of a maelstrom. The conductor search committee had him on a giddying whirl of panels, interviews, media appearances, social events and rehearsals.

He met with orchestra members, symphony staff, union reps, board members, patrons, socialites, and even briefly with Bill Viertel, affectionately known to the musicians as Quarternote. The squirrely little man was autistic. He supposedly had an incredible knowledge of Beethoven but not much else. "He's a homeless guy, kind of our adopted mascot," whispered one of the musicians showing Petrie around on his first visit to Davies Hall.

Today Quarternote was helping with the coffee service as yet another group of interrogators filed into a conference room. He was well-padded, wearing multiple layers of clothing.

"Napoleon," he said to Petrie. A surprisingly-deep monotone. Petrie heard a muddied F sharp. "Hero then zero. Napoleon, Napoleon." Petrie drew back.

"Quarternote isn't talking about you, Jamison," laughed Gunnar Thorsen. "He's referring to the 'Eroica'. Isn't that right, Bill? I believe Beethoven planned on dedicating the Third Symphony to Napoleon. Then changed his mind."

Quarternote nodded, almost ritually. "Yes. True. Eroica, yes. Opus 55. Napoleon dropped." Carefully, Quarternote drew steaming coffee into a china cup, seated it on a saucer and handed it to a well-perfumed woman in furs. "E-flat. Favorite key. Beethoven's. Mine."

Thorson grinned. "Not that you might not be a bit of a Napoleon, eh, Jamison?" But maybe that's what we need in a conductor?" Thorsen was head of the search committee. Petrie had quickly sized him up as a two-faced schmoozer. A familiar enough type.

Introductions, then another round of grilling. Petrie was struggle to put Helen out of his mind. And Alex. Focus was imperative. These people were especially sharp.

Judge Lombard, a petite brunette with unusually large dark eyes, led off with questions about the business side of music. Petrie talked about Bellevue's success but deferred directly taking credit. He turned up the refined knob on his accent.

"As for here, you have an extremely-competent staff. I'd depend on each of them. It's all balance. A matter of close cooperation between the artistic and the practical." He looked around the room. "I can manage convoluted time signatures with the best of them, but I can't add two and two. So I'm smart enough to rely on an expert staff for fiscal matters." He earned a few chuckles.

As the group laughed, his mind wandered to Lake Union. He pulled himself back by staring at the gold-decorated top of City Hall, visible outside the window. *Gilt and guilt. My frequent companions.*

He fielded the expected questions about his showmanship, musicianship, programming philosophy. Someone asked about his propensity for changing the music. He was known for interpreting many works with considerable freedom, unusual tempos, extreme dynamic contrasts.

"Purists aren't happy," he said, looking directly at a bleak-faced man. *Boris Karloff.* "But audiences are delighted." He turned to the woman in furs, giving her a silent cue.

"And audiences mean money," she informed everyone.

As the session neared its end, another admiring matron, cheeks glowing with rouge and blushes, asked if he preferred to conduct with a baton or with hands alone.

Talk about stupid non sequiturs. Petrie rewarded her with his biggest melt-them smile. He told her it depended on what the players wanted, the size of the hall, many other factors."If you'll indulge me," he said, "I'll tell you a brief baton story." He always earned points with a few of his charming anecdotes.

He'd been leading the Bellevue Philharmonic in Beethoven's Ninth. During a furious allegro, the baton slipped from his grasp and flew backwards into the audience. He continued conducting with his hands. In his peripheral vision he saw that a little boy of no more than ten had seized the baton, clambered over the front seats and now stood at the edge of the stage, close to the podium, holding up the baton, uncertain what to do next.

"Without losing the proverbial beat," Petrie said, "I knelt slightly, swept my arm backwards and down, took the baton from his hand, swooped into a dramatic upbeat, and the show went on. Happy Beethoven. Proud little boy. Amused audience."

"And more money?" said Boris Karloff, dryly. *Hm. Maybe that story was a bit too self-serving. On the other hand, they want flash and personality.*

The panel wrapped up with pleasantries. Petrie shook hands in the hallway, thinking ahead to tonight's rehearsal. He wondered if he'd correctly picked up the signals from the second oboist. *Eyes of a tiger shark.*

Thorsen took his elbow, drew him aside and quietly said a few people had an additional point to address. He led Petrie to an adjacent room. Four board members stood there, two men and two women. All looked slightly uncomfortable. But dangerous. *A circling pod of orcas.*

God, how could they know about Helen? Petrie found himself sweating.

Old Mr. Ghirardelli, who'd said little in the main gathering, cleared his throat. "We've heard a rumor." "He cleared this throat again. "Well, actually we have it on reasonable authority, that you've made some rather... inappropriate remarks about Victoria d'Milano."

With difficulty, Petrie kept his face neutral.. *d'Milano? It's not about Helen?* He managed to raise a slightly-puzzled eyebrow. *'Reasonable authority?' Escher the saboteur.*

Maestro

Mrs. Figueroa was talking. Petrie juggled confusion with relief. The woman's emerald earrings glistened, bobbing in 6/8 time. "We're pretty liberal in the Bay Area, but there is a limit."

"So how do you respond?" asked Thorsen, showing his less benign face. A moray eel flashing perfect teeth. Petrie didn't hesitate. "Dr. d'Milano is an excellent musician and a fine conductor. I respect her work. Immensely. *Here goes.* I also think she's a very attractive woman. Who wouldn't?"

"Beside the point," said Barrington Lakes, studying well-manicured nails. "Our source said you made comments about her, em, posterior. You may have a free-spirited private life—and, yes, the public may enjoy some of that—but..." He couldn't look Petrie in the eye.

"...but we think our conductors should show respect," said Thorsen. "A phrase like 'cute ass' is out of line, wouldn't you say?"

"I beg your pardon. 'Cute ass'?" *Escher's trying for checkmate in one.* "I don't know who told you that, but I never said any such thing. *God, I hope he wasn't recording.* And I never would. But apart from that misinformation, I'm sure you'll agree any personal peccadillos are less important than musical credentials. Less important than leadership skills, innovation, showmanship. And I think you'll agree I have those in spades."

"Oh, you do, you do," blurted Mrs. Figueroa, immediately reddening. Petrie had the urge to add "I have a cute ass at the podium too." He could almost read that thought in her eyes. But he simply gave a modest smile.

Judge Lombard studied him for a moment. "All right, then, I think that's taken care of. End of sidebar." She began buttoning her coat. "Have a good rehearsal. I hear you're keeping the orchestra on its toes."

Crazy-haired, Dabby sat on the front of the music stand, watching the rehearsal. He peered over the edge at the violas.

Petrie had raced to his hotel, responded to a text from Alex, showered, nibbled a sandwich. Shaking off uneasy vibes from the interview, but failing to put aside guilt over Helen, he'd dashed back to the hall. After ten minutes of deep breathing in his dressing room, he'd calmed enough to ascend the podium, resplendently casual.

"Right. Ladies and gentlemen. It's time for the proof of the pudding or the tip of the icing on the cake. Forgive me. I make music, not metaphors."

There was laughter. The second oboist had a sunlit smile. Aimed at him.

"Since I only have you today and Wednesday before we make San Francisco rock..." (more laughter), "Mr. Ortega has agreed we'll start with the Bruch."

The soloist trotted out. The musicians thumped their stands.

"Of course," said Petrie," we're actually doing it first so Ramon can escape to watch the Giants game." Laughter. Ortega pumped his fist. "Some kind of cricket, I believe?" More laughter. Then everyone quickly settled.

Maestro

As usual, Petrie could focus on the music, critically listen, glance at the score, give cues, attend to the soloist, make adjustments, suggest nuances, and still have room for extraneous thoughts. Complete heightened awareness. One of the joys of conducting. Once again in command of all, he could see all. A grease spot on a violist's shirt. A cellist chewing gum, working it against the principal rhythm. Two other cellists sweating. A wildly-colored shopping bag lolling at someone's tapping feet. *Tapping. Bad form.* One of the first violinists wore a very short skirt. Was she teasing him? *Has to wait. Alex arrives soon. Damn, I wonder if Helen...*

In his career, he realized, he'd had at least one lover from each major orchestra section. *Enough to form a chamber group.* He smiled broadly. The concertmaster, glancing up, took it as approval, half-nodded.

Ortega finished a bravura passage, flourished the bow. Petrie tilted his head in acknowledgement. *Don't try to upstage me, you bastard. It's my audition.*

With a dramatic gesture of his own, Petrie cued the winds. The first clarinetist had slicked-back hair. Supercool, an aloof barracuda. The orchestra was awash in fat-lipped puffers and puckering wrasses, a whiskered goatfish, a Dali-mustached trigger fish. Schools of tiny needlefish darted up and down, violin bows changing direction. Bassists' arms swung in unison, sea grasses swaying. Over there that odd little man Quarternote hovered in the wings, hunched like a hermit crab, pincers moving. *Lord, is he conducting?*

Petrie cued the flutes. He remembered one Hartford flutist and her incredible tonguing technique, beautifully transferred to playing a very different instrument. *Enough already.*

"Jolly good. But can we please take that passage again. Much more rubato?"

At the break, Quarternote helped with refreshments. He handed Petrie an unasked-for cup of tea and muttered "Freude, Freude, Maestro."

"Danke. We'll get to the joys of Herr Beethoven soon. You like the Third?"

The little man nodded nervously, his gaze darting somewhere far beyond Petrie. "Three. Five. Nine. Favorites. I study every one." He clicked his words, a typewriter.

"Quarternote knows more about Beethoven than anyone," said the concertmaster, slurping coffee. "No offense, Mr. Petrie."

"None taken. I'm sure he does." Petrie saw the second oboist looking at him. She nibbled a cookie. Slowly.

When Petrie got back to the hotel, Alex was sitting by the window, sipping Pernod. She was en route to Japan for a major shoot. "Gonna be a tough one," she said. "'Faces of Fukushima'. It's got to be so raw for many of those people. Maybe forever raw."

Petrie poured himself a whiskey. "God yes. And kids too? Will you photograph kids?"

Alex stood up. "My editors expect it. But I'm trying not to think about that now." Lithe, sensual, she stared out the window. "So, JP. Is San Francisco going to be our next stop? Little cable cars and all those stars and bars?"

"Hard to tell. I think they like me, but they're a tough bunch. I'm giving it my best."

"And that's a lot, isn't it?" Alex said. She put down her drink. "Well, I've only got the one night here."

They stood close together at the large window, looking down at the scattered lights of the city. The LED sculpture on the Bay Bridge twinkled. Electric fish wriggled between the spans. Quicksilver raindrops slid down dark silver spires.

Coit Tower, pale and small in contrast, stood proud and erect. The dark shape of Alcatraz both beckoned and menaced.

"Much of life's a prison," she said, reading his thoughts. "You do what you can to break free."

"You think marriage is a prison?"

"Not ours. At least not the way we play it."

"Yeah." He saw Helen's pale face reflected in the window. "Not the way we play it." He gulped the last of his whiskey.

Alex took his hand. He smelled jasmine. "Makes these times seem like assignations. Illicit. More exciting. Who needs a conventional marriage? That really is a prison." She led him toward the bedroom.

Petrie was naked, diving for pearls in the clearest water he'd even known. Three banded damselfish swam alongside. A dark Achilles tang darted close. Its gills flashed white. Its tail flicked. A large spot rippled. An orange teardrop. Petrie blinked and saw Alex beside him in the half-light. She was leaning on one arm, watching him.

"You awake?" He blinked again, managed a nod.

"Jamie, about the question of children. Shh. I've been thinking. A lot. You know I need my freedom. I'm selfish. But it's more than that. Wherever I go, I see tragedy, despair. I'm talking about the kids I encounter. They fill my lens with sorrow, Jamie. So many in pain. Growing up damaged, if they grow up at all. Damaged kids, damaged adults, damaged world. I don't want to bring more children into this."

Even in the dim light, Petrie saw that her eyes were wet. He started to respond, but she cut him off.

"So it's this way. I don't want to take any more chances. I've decided to have my tubes tied. I'm scheduled when I get back from Kyoto. It's not reversible."

"'Lex...'lex...'" For once, he was at a loss for words. *Not reversible? The procedure? The decision?* "Hold it!" He struggled to concentrate. "Can we talk about this? Once you're home? You can't...You don't..."

"Oh, Jamie, this is such a difficult one. But it's my choice." She stroked his hair. "There's really no more to be said."

He closed his eyes again. Dark colors swirled, silverblue tracers flashed past, deep reds pulsed and vortexed. Petrie shivered. The room seemed very cold.

Musically, the dress rehearsal was going beautifully. The orchestra was fully his. He led his arrangement of the Stravinsky through extra twists and turns. It was like combining San Francisco's crookedest street with a monkey puzzle tree. The Bruch was stunning. Petrie was confident he was scoring lots of points. Dabby, at his feet on the podium, positively beamed.

But throughout, even in the most complex moments, Alex haunted Petrie. He thought he saw her among shadowy figures in the wings. *More diminuendo.* He could hear her voice in the middle harmonies. *Cue the bassoons* She was so jittery about kids.. There had to be other things underlying her feelings. Maybe her parents' death. Some related fear. *Hold back the crescendo. Hold, hold, make them scream for the climax. Yes!* And why did Helen's abortion upset him? There was no way... *Sostenuto. That's it. Ah, perfect!* He thought how everything seemed to be about tension and release. So easy to handle on the podium. Elsewhere was a different matter.

Intermission allowed little respite. He rethought the last minutes with Alex, her taxi rumbling impatiently at the curb. She wouldn't even promise to think about things. She was affectionate, even loving, but she remained firm. This very moment she was on her way to Japan. He imagined the depths beneath the streaking jet, had to stop himself when he thought of her parents' plane, disintegrating, settling to the bottom. *Tubes tied? What's she doing?*

And there was Helen. By now she would have, must have... He wished he'd taken more time to think. He snorted. The time to really think was before he let his libido conduct his actions. But now. *Goddammit.* He found he was increasingly angry at himself.

The stage manager called the end of the intermission.

Petrie came out of his dressing room and almost bumped into Quarternote. The man seemed more agitated than his usual nervousness. Petrie nodded and headed toward the stage. Quarternote scurried after him, trying to say something.

"Tempo," he finally managed. "He says adagio assai. You are too fast. Not right."

Petrie kept walking. "Are you talking about the Beethoven?"

Quarternote was sweating. *Wearing too many layers. Challenging the conductor, more like. Guy's got balls.* "Beethoven, yes Beethoven. Second movement. Quaver at 80. No faster."

They reached stage right. Many of the players were drifting out to their places. Petrie heard retuning, fragments of the Beethoven tossed about. Slivers of other works. Little musical jokes. *Let's be clever. See how I turn Mozart into the Beatles. Let's get started; I've got a hot date.*

He stopped. "Look, I need to go. Thanks for the comments."

Quarternote shook his head. "I studied it. Funeral march. Not a dance. Tempo, maestro, please. Tempo. Tempo."

Petrie glared at the man. The quivering little face looked up at him. Innocent. Not defiant. But it annoyed him greatly. "Look, you bloody little twerp. Who do you think you are?"

Several musicians glanced at the pair, frowning. Quarternote didn't react to the insult. "I know Beethoven," he repeated. "Tempos perfect. Perfect markings."

"Listen, chum. Beethoven was a syphilitic boor, the last person to tell me how to interpret his work. So sod off. And sod your tempos."

Quarternote trembled, moved his head wildly, scampered off, a squirrel. He stopped, hesitated, started back, turned again and dashed toward an emergency exit. Bleating "Eroica! Eroica!" he hit the crash bar and plunged out.

An alarm clanged. Petrie winced. Unplanned dissonance.

Most of the orchestra seemed unaware of the confrontation. The Third Symphony went brilliantly. Petrie, immersed, thought of himself moving like a danseur. He felt like a master sculptor, shaping the sonic clay. An alchemist, creating fountains of gold from ink and paper.

During the second movement he felt only a tiny twinge of guilt. He led it his way, at his tempo.

He was in his dressing room, reliving the onstage congratulations. An excellent dress. Next up, the big night. He'd make the public performance even better. He thought about the second fugato and decided he could make more dramatic use of the basses. He decided to stylize more cues. To hold the finale back even more then take it flying. He thought distractedly of Alex, far over the Pacific. There was a knock. Uninvited, someone opened the door.

A striking middle-aged woman stepped in. She looked tense. A horn player, he remembered. Third horn. Great tone. Up close, great in every other department. *No, no no. Enough to deal with.* "May I help you?"

"Sorry to interrupt, Mr. Petrie. They thought you should know. Bill Viertel—the gentleman we call Quarternote—was hit by a taxi. Just outside the hall. While we were rehearsing."

"Quarternote? Good God. How is he?"

"In serious condition, apparently. Intensive care. San Francisco General. The manager is headed over there. Asked me to tell you. We know Quarternote really admires you." She swiveled and left.

Petrie puzzled over her tone. Irony? Disapproval? Anger? Whatever it was, it triggered a strong jolt of guilt. A feeling becoming very familiar.

Despite a strong breeze, the air by the bay was warm. Petrie smelled tar, eucalyptus, brine. Something decaying. He wrinkled his nose.

The greenblack waters teemed with white sails. Weekend sailors competing for space. So much was about competition. Petrie felt uneasy. Felt less than on top of things. Not his norm. He chewed again over the conductor contest, gnawed at other things competing in his life. *Very little control. Suddenly very little control.*

He resumed walking. Framing the west, the Golden Gate Bridge dazzled, perfect in form, suspended grace. *A symphony. No ordinary architect. Had to be a musician, a master.* It took obsession to reach perfection in anything. Maybe to the point of craziness. Obsessed and crazy, you can throw huge spans over impossibly empty air, scribble music of new power, triumph over obstacles.

Fucking deaf. Beethoven was going deaf when he wrote the Eroica. Facing deafness and contemplating suicide. Somehow turning it all around. *Reaching for greatness across the span of centuries.*

Gulls floated, dove, screeched at each other, sullied the water's edge with flurries of white and gray. Petrie stopped to watch two young children flinging popcorn. The gulls rushed in, squawking, fearless, devouring. The girl leapt back, terrified, delighted. The boy stood resolute, hurling popcorn into the wind. On the path, their mother laughed.

Petrie thought of himself barefoot on the rippled Blackpool sand, trousers rolled, pail and spade in hand. A rare trip to the seaside from landlocked Belper. His mother and father stood on the walkway, stiff and incongruous in their Marks and Spencer finery, waiting for Jimmy to finish his allotted time. He waved to them. He thought his mother was waving back, but saw she was adjusting her hat. His father pulled out a pocket watch, stared at it.

The gulls screeched. "Eroica!" *No sense of pitch.* Petrie thought about Quarternote. Child, innocent, savant. And now savaged by a vehicle.

He tried not to blame himself. But he knew his thoughtlessness had a lot to do with it. And something else nagged. "How would either of us know how to be a parent?" Alex asked. "There's only one option," said Helen. "Well, then," Judge Lombard pronounced. "End of sidebar."

The breeze picked up. The boy and girl chattered to their mother. Petrie watched them walk off, bounding like rabbits. He pulled out his cell phone and called his manager in Seattle.

Davies Hall was filled. Over 2,000 San Franciscans were ready to sit in judgment on Candidate Number Four, one Jamison Petrie.

The house monitor in his dressing room buzzed with excitement. Petrie stood before the mirror, perfecting his hair and fine-tuning his tux. *No loose studs. Not tonight.* He felt like a gladiator in the dark tunnel, seconds before walking into the daylight to face a moment of truth. Would it be lions or slaves? Bloody battle or easy pickings? Thumbs up or thumbs down? He laughed uneasily. Escher and the rest were hoping he'd fall. This might not be so easy.

In the wings he straightened his shoulders, waited for a moment longer. At last he strode onto the stage, assaulted by blinding light and robust applause. The hall smelled of carnations, polished wood, and—what was that?—old money?

Dabby was discreetly sitting at a bottom corner of the podium. This was one concert he couldn't miss. Petrie acknowledged the orchestra, bounded up, took his place, raised his arms, made eye contact with the winds, gave the downbeat for the Stravinsky. *Off we go.*

Within moments, something felt different. The notes were exact, the sonorities exquisite, the rhythms engagingly complex. His own orchestration was taking Stravinsky's piece into a new realm. But there was something. *What?* He led them into an astonishing passage with tympani and bassoons leapfrogging over rich chords from the strings. And right then he understood. The audience couldn't possibly detect it, but Petrie felt it. The orchestra was not yielding to him. Under that professional surface lurked an angry pushback.

He brought in the brass. Perfect entrance, luscious intonation, but he felt resentment. The cellos bit at him. The flutes sneered under sweetness. Even the triangle had sardonic overtones. The clang of an alarm. And it hit him. Quarternote. *God, the whole damn orchestra's in payback mode.* That wasn't adulation he saw in their intent faces. It was vitriol.

They had reached the first of many passages of fiercely difficult cross-rhythms and harmonic minefields. Petrie threw his full attention into the work. He didn't come up for air until the end. Astounding, the solid applause, given the battle he had just fought with the orchestra.

During the Bruch, the musicians yielded considerably. Petrie knew this had nothing to do with him, everything to do with wanting to support Ramon Ortega. Petrie took full advantage and led a sumptuous performance. Ortega and his Stradivarius were inspired.

As the last movement ended and the applause poured toward them, Petrie tried to catch the eye of his second oboist. She was absorbed by a tiny moth fluttering above her head.

Intermission was a lifetime of solitude. Prematurely soaked, Petrie changed clothes. He sat alone in his dressing room thinking about Alex, her passion, her amazing creative eye, her stubbornness. About Helen, her odd mixture of fire and sweetness, her tough independence. They both pushed back, just as the orchestra had. Challenge and punishment.

He badly wanted to go diving, seek release. He closed his eyes and focused on the Third Symphony. As he thought through the second movement a strong image played through his mind. On a path in the woods near Heiligenstadt, Quarternote bounced along beside Beethoven. Both wore long morning coats trailing near the ground. Both wore crushed top hats and tattered cravats. Beethoven, glowering, but attentive, had his hands clasped behind his back. Quarternote was doing all the talking.

The oboe's plaint. Swelling tuning sounds. The three minute call. Petrie went to the side of the stage and stood beside a staff assistant. The hall hummed. Petrie, still musing about the image he'd seen, asked the assistant about Quarternote's condition. She whispered that Bill was stable and improving surprisingly quickly. Visitors were now OK. But no flowers. The dear little man was allergic.

It was time. Petrie walked on stage to substantial applause. He gave the audience an exaggerated 19th century bow. The musicians rapped their stands in salute. He couldn't read anything into that. Tradition required it. *Fifty minutes, give or take.*

He quickly realized the orchestra had not resumed being his friend. From the opening measures, the subsurface tension swirled about him, an unyielding current. He had to pull together all his resources to retain control. The emerging sound was perfect, but he knew there was an increasing danger of this being professional but soulless.

His own anger and resentment almost caught up with him. He pushed and pulled. He fought insane images of Napoleon trying to rally obstinate troops. The tension almost dragged him under.

Suddenly he yielded to the music. Quarternote and Beethoven stopped walking, looked at him. He sent a silent message to the orchestra. *If you won't do this for me, do it for them.* It was all about the music. He slipped into his zone. The friction suddenly produced sparks. Petrie dove into the players' rebukes and redirected them into passion. The first movement shone with increased brilliance.

He took the second movement in a sweeping elastic arc, mixing tempos between his own and those Quarternote wanted, pushing gently against the orchestra to get original effects. Echoes of a New Orleans street band funeral danced in the background.

The scherzo rippled with new vigor. Petrie saw Beethoven and Quarternote vanish into the woods, skipping in time.

In the finale, he pushed hard against the musicians, and created an edgy playfulness. He used their resistance to add fresh energy to the fugue. He turned their remaining reluctance to exciting effects in the closing, building and holding and building and holding, till the symphony at last burst in victory.

There was a sudden vacuum. Silence. Not a cough, not a rustle, not a word. Petrie realized the tension had produced a remarkable concert. *Not the kind of interplay I'd ever want again.*

The applause came at tsunami strength. He brought the orchestra to standing and turned to accept the first wave. As he stepped backwards, his heel kicked Dabby, who spiraled off the podium. Somehow the little bear landed upright, facing the audience, his wild hair haloed by a spotlight, his dark eyes staring at Petrie's back.

A bit dazed, Petrie accepted the ovation. Musically, he realized, his candidacy was a triumph. In other areas, who could guess? The Quarternote factor: unknown. But for better or worse, it was over. Except for the waiting.

The echoing, fluorescent hallways of San Francisco General were a shock after the elegance of Davies Hall. *Chronicle* pages lay strewn about a table in the crowded waiting room. Petrie hunted. A small headline read "Exceptional Performance." Not bad, given it was on page 20. He reread the review while waiting his turn to visit progressive care. Praise was an aphrodisiac, even if it had a short half-life.

Petrie had expected to smell disinfectant, formaldehyde, odors of poorly-hidden sickness. Instead, he was teased by the smell of rainwet asphalt and ripe strawberries.

And now lilies. A muttering woman juggling a huge bouquet and a dripping umbrella sagged into a chair beside him.

At last he was allowed in. Two patients dozed as weary watchers sat by their beds. A sallow man attempted a smile as a tall woman hovered over him. She seemed to be wielding a baton.

"Ginger ale. Drink up, Bob." It was a straw. "Good for you."

Quarternote's bed was jammed in a back corner. The small man was propped almost upright, disappearing amid bandages and medical paraphernalia.

Petrie couldn't guess what reaction he'd get, but he stepped right to the bedside. Quarternote was awake, blinking in discomfort.

"Hello, Mr. Viertel. Remember me?"

Quarternote turned his head slightly, blinked again. "Yes. Guest conductor. Napoleon." The low voice rasped. No animosity. No fear. No affect at all.

"That's right. Napoleon. Jamison Petrie. How are you? I'm so sorry about what happened." Did he mean the incident or the taxi? He wasn't sure.

"Music does not happen here."

"I'm sorry. Look, do you remember our last conversation?"

"No." One eye was bloodshot, the other runny. Petrie hadn't noticed the tic before.

"I was rude, very rude. I want to make it up to you."

Quarternote stared, a cypher. Monitors beeped. The ginger ale patient slurped through his straw.

Petrie opened the small FedEx box he'd brought, withdrew the package, unwrapped it carefully.

"I had my manager send this from Seattle. I want to you to have it." He handed the vellum to Quarternote, who hesitated, then took it.

"Do you know what it is?" Petrie trembled as released the score. He wasn't sure if it was reverence or regret. Or both.

Quarternote turned a page. "Funfte? The Fifth?" His eyes widened. "Old?"

"Really old. When this was printed, Beethoven was still alive."

Quarternote grimaced with what might have been a gleam of recognition. He turned another page. "Dadada da!" he whispered. "Dadada da!"

"Yes. Beethoven called it 'Fate knocking at the door'. Oh, but you probably know that. I think he was spot on. Anyway, it's yours."

"Mine?"

"It's yours. The score is for you to keep."

There was no thank you. Maybe a bit of a distorted smile. Petrie had never noticed how few teeth the man had.

Quarternote disappeared into the music, nodding. Petrie stood there, uncomfortable. After a moment, he offered his hand. Quarternote remained oblivious. Petrie lightly touched him on the shoulder. No response.

As Petrie crossed the room, Quarternote began humming and muttering. He conducted with one thin hand. His red hospital bracelet slid up and down his wrist.

In the lobby, Petrie passed several of the orchestra's musicians. He assumed they were going up to see Quarternote. They nodded but didn't stop to talk. He couldn't read anything in their eyes.

He walked outside into the light rain, looked up, let the drops wash his face.

Night descended at a perfect andante, slowly inking away the fading colors of sunset.

Petrie was again in the velvet thrall of the Caribbean. He was diving off the coast of Bonaire. The exotic mass of South America pulled at him, the gravity of continents.

Alex was still in Japan. Helen was who knew where. His future lay in the hands of the San Francisco committee. Dark waters surrounded him.

It would be at least three weeks before any decision. He planned to spend one of them on this desert island. Earlier he'd watched stately pink flamingos slowly marching in the salt ponds. Souza in bird time. He'd seen fat iguanas staring out to sea from their rocky perches, lords of the sun. Their impenetrable features reminded him of Thorsen. *How do you second-guess a goodbye handshake?*

He surfaced to orient himself. A short distance away, long blue streaks glowed and rippled the calm water. The rest of his group was experimenting with blue fluorescent torches. *Darth Vaders waving their light swords, disturbing the night life.* He preferred to explore alone. He turned, found the shore beacons exactly where they should be, and slowly descended into the shadows.

In the increasing blackness, he listened to bubbles, to his heartbeat, to the deep croaking of a frog fish. Not a bad sound. Better than an over-the-hill baritone he remembered conducting in Beethoven's Ninth.

Beethoven. *Fate knocks at the door.*

He switched on his flashlight and swept it gently over the bottom. Parrot fish slept on their sides, cocooned in mucus, concert dowagers dozing in pale turquoise wraps. Crabs fed methodically, moving their claws up and down, timpanists in syncopation.

On impulse, he conducted with his light. A myriad miniscule creatures thronged through the beam. Small striped fish fled his upbeat. Swarms of little red worms roiled in a frantic contradance. Tumbling.

Alex, the Golden Gate, Quarternote, Helen. All tumbled, tumbled and turned, turned and churned.

Enough.

He descended, floated just above the bottom. He extinguished the light. The intense counterpoint vanished. He settled quietly in one spot, blind. Weightless. Thinking.

His vision adjusted. Suddenly in front, above, all around him was magic. Light.

Maestro

Bioluminescent strings of pearls glittered and twinkled. Tiny crustaceans, ostracods signaling love and desire. Long filaments of passion and hope. Multitudes of ocean fireflies holding hands, gone joyously mad. He exhaled. His bubbles flashed and glimmered. He moved his hands. Thousands of sparkles spiraled, blue and white teardrops cascaded and spun. Enveloped in a shimmering softness, he drifted in deep space, floated among galaxies, conducted a million stars.

Undertow

These were no ordinary leaves. Skeletonic fingers raked across the wind-tortured shingles. Brittle dancers tapped maniacally over the roof, pirouetting insanely and noisily along the gutters.

Pacing in her living room, Cassie shivered.

Boom!

The ocean again scoured the blowhole, tried to tear it apart. She could sense the raging spoutspray violating the autumn evening.

The wind savaged the panes. Coveys of chattering leaves flew up and staccatoed across the glass, demanding admission.

Boom!

Tonight the pace was demonic. The Pacific trying to shake off its name. Cassie's headache accelerated. She loved the blowhole, their own geologic secret, the centerpiece of a cabal of caves below their property. But tonight the deep poundings were harsh and spiteful heartbeats.

Cassie opened the door, pushing against an irritated gust, stepped outside. The tang of ozone, wood smoke, dying leaves and shore brine rushed to assail her.

Boom!

Even from up here Cassie could hear the hiss of the spray falling back into the waves, disappointed. No escape. There's never an escape. Whatever passage you choose, the end is the same. You plummet to oblivion.

The wind, mischievous, shifted, dropped. Gulls arced across the golden streak above the silhouetting trees.

Marc had found this place. "It's not Mendocino," he said. "But it can be ours." Well, technically it would be paid for by Cassie's inheritance, but she wanted to share everything.

The first time he brought her here, Marc drove his strident little red MG up the coast road with frightening skill, rocketed past Sea Ranch, terrorized the locals of Gualala and Point Arena. Somewhere, many twisting miles above Albion, he slewed seaward, raced down a long hidden track and roared to a stop at the edge of a small bluff. Their thick dusty wake swirled over them and careened out to sea. Sunning pelicans arose, disgruntled, beat a dignified retreat.

Cassie clambered out, horrified from the ride, delighted with what she found. She and Marc wandered, he leading the way. The warm air offered her seaweed, clover, pine. Hidden birds gossiped intimately about the intruders. Turkey vultures creased the sky, scanned the earth for fresh mortality.

The setting was magnificently private. The weathered cedar cottage huddled into the slight slope. The rooms were cozy but filled with light.

Cassie gazed out the front window. A stand of leaning junipers parted graciously to provide a shimmering sea view. The ocean was a bluegray sheen.

They explored outdoors, soon clambering over the edge of the furrowed bluff. They discovered that the home had its own tiny secluded cove, awash in bobbing kelp heads. Or were those sea lions? A moment of laughter at ignorance, innocence. Marc charged ahead, and Cassie followed him out onto one of the rocky battlements guarding the cove. She looked down at the base of the opposite cliff and grinned.

"I think there are caves!" she yelled into the breeze. Her hair whipped her face. Sharp stonepoints probed the soles of her sandals.

"Wow!" said Marc. "Look at this!"

A large blowhole gaped on the flattest part of the rocks, its shadowy maw drooling seawater. More than big enough to tumble through. Cassie stood back a bit, but Marc strode right to the edge.

The ocean shot up a flare of spume to greet them. Marc retreated, wet, hooting.

"Drop down there, you'd be a goner. Dragged all the way to Japan. If you weren't crushed or drowned first. Great! And this is ours, baby! No tourists ever. Ours!"

He was assuming the purchase as a fait accompli. But she knew she wanted it too. Wanted him.

"Let's take the plunge!" she giggled.

Marc rewarded her with his trademark smile and turned to study the promised land. Cassie edged closer to the blowhole. A small white butterfly meandered over the opening. From underneath came a rush, a snarl, surging thunder. Fat, briny tendrils reached up, enmeshed the unwary creature, held it high in split-second triumph. Then the dark grasp of gravity dragged wave, foam and insect into the slurping abyss. A watery crash. Gurgling. Fizzing. A wet whisper.

Boom!

Cassie stood in the near-twilight glow, staring toward the darkening ocean, inhaling that strange autumnal mix of decay and fecundity. She shifted slightly and stepped on a tense collusion of leaves. Curling veins of death crunched, sighed.

What had happened in the time since she first set foot here? All that joy, dizzying weekends of fixing up, moving in, racing along the coast, adventures in the little towns, birding at Bodega Bay, incredible oysters at Tony's, cedar baths at Osmosis, sticky buns from Wild Flour, rainy day forays to Copperfield's—loading up for long, lazy reads by the cottage fire. Touch as soft as champagne bubbles.

Abalone shell skies by day, white moonshards on the sea at night. Promises. A future. Offshore: enchantingly eerie fog banks. At home: unclouded horizons.

Boom!

Love had drained away like the tide edge receding on sand—wet to dry; there, not-there. Life was erosion, illusion.

Now she was lost in the catacombs of grief. Haunted by what was, what should have been. By what had happened.

When underpinnings corrode, expectance collapses into cruel surprise. Life, like the sea, can blindside you.

One afternoon, Marc, beachcombing on his own, found something. Someone. She was an oceanographer or a biologist. Something. From Santa Rosa or

Petaluma. Somewhere. When he finally told Cassie, she took in the words but only heard the swirling pain.

Boom!

Marc, restless as the ocean. They were out on the rocks—their rocks—watching sea lions in the cove—real ones, not kelp, she'd laughed, but Marc didn't react. He seemed distracted. No, feverish. He stood near their blowhole. A huge geyser exploded. Cassie turned to watch.

As the water sizzled and drained through crevices, Marc, drenched, slipping on wet granite, blurted out his betrayal. Her blood drained through the fissures of her soul.

She couldn't remember what she'd said—what she'd screamed. Or what she'd done.

Boom!

This time a sodden bass. The wind had shifted. She smelled damp wood burning, rotting seaweed. The air was gritty, the skies dulling gold.

Her headache a whirlpool of complaint, Cassie picked her way through fallen branches to the bluff. The dry clifftop grasses clung together, rustled nervously. The ocean was heavy with graywhite swells.

Cassie stumbled onto the rocks. Something rough and spiky pushed hard, cut through her left sandal. She felt sticky moisture trickle along her foot.

Boom!

Oddly, the sound seemed more muted out here, but now she could see the spreading upspray, jeweled by long remnants of sunlight. Slowly she squished to the blowhole, going close. Closer. Closer still. Spray blew into her face, stinging, coarse. Icy.

At the edge, she peered down. A trick of reflection splayed light fragments throughout the shaft. Jagged stone knuckles dripped. Ebony scarfaces seeped. Far below, past brutal stalactites and oozing sidespikes, the impatient surf frothed, heaved, sought freedom.

Then it pulsed, lurched, reared.

Boom!

Cassie lunged back as the angry upsurge vomited skyward. It burst all around, completely soaking her.

I need cleansing, she thought.

Trembling, she inched again to the edge and stared into the seething void.

Not just grief. Guilt. The black, dank caverns of guilt. What was she capable of, she wondered. Misjudgment? Yes. Failure? Yes. Something else?

Below, the waters churned, muttered. Forgiving? Complicit? Beckoning? Cassie agonized.

The wind pushed at her. The fall evening, exhausted, slid into night.

Birds of Prey

The room, small and windowless, could be claustrophobic. But Bryce has found it to be stimulating, a place from which he can command the earth.

The dream, open and limitless, should be freeing. But for Bryce, inevitably, it turns frightening, suffocating.

Day after day, the two—the room and the dream—come together, feed upon each other.

Bryce's room is far out in the desert, part of a cluster of trailers eyed only by the relentless sun and a few covert satellites. Blank-faced boxes, blotchy with camouflage paint. Some little more than shipping crates perched on jack wheels.

None has a window. But inside, monitors reveal the world. Inside, men and women change the world.

If you spend long hours in these dark rooms, no matter how ordinary your own home when you return to it, you may twist and turn in your sleep, hunting for daylight, for air. If you spend long hours in these rooms doing what you excel at, it's very possible your dreams may try to shred your soul.

Bryce's dreams forever plummet into nightmares.

Almost always they begin with the same magnificent prelude, the same startling transformation.

A great blue heron, first a huge silent shadow, then a sudden soft fuselage, slategray and flashing rust, drops over the roof and commands the pond, shoving aside astonished lilies, spearing aghast goldfish one by one, taking leisurely, insolent flight when Bryce open the door.

Instantly Bryce becomes the heron, soaring freely over rugged Idaho rangelands, with slow sensuous beating of long wings, following a weary stream, sharp eyes patrolling smudgy dots of sage on the cracked brown earth.

When exhilaration shatters, Bryce is the drone, the predator, the reaper. The sere and bumpy landscape, resolutely mountainous, is now very much like Afghanistan or Pakistan. He flies with terrible speed and singular, deadly purpose, controlled by some power far behind his unflinching eyes.

Sometimes he is lucky and awakes before the hellfire in his belly shoots forward on a pitiless trajectory of devastation. Sometimes.

His wife isn't very sympathetic. "It's no dream, Bry. We gotta take care of that damn heron." She fondles his top uniform button. "And it's your job to fly those pretend planes. You're keeping us all safe. Go get 'em, tiger."

Bryce knows the party line. Mostly he subscribes to it. With his superb aviation and computer skills, piloting unmanneds is second nature to him. He flies them from a soft leather chair in an air-conditioned trailer overflowing with high-tech gear. The only attempts at décor: a frayed sports banner and a melancholy rubber plant. No masks, no chutes, no ejection systems. And no hostile fire.

Except for the dreams. They are the enemy, firing at him nightly. They tear into him brutally, making him gasp and sweat. Making him doubt.

This morning, no dream, the real heron descended at dawn, performed a reconnaissance, stabbed a fleeing frog, flipped it into the air and gulletted it with unblinking indifference, moments later rising to the west with serene majesty, Bryce frozen in place at the kitchen window. He thinks it fortunate that his wife is still asleep.

The image still lingers as Bryce leaves the late afternoon briefing and settles into the cramped trailer cockpit beside his sensor operator, a redheaded captain. She nods to him and continues muttering into her headset microphone. There's no smile on her freckled face. She's already awash in data. The room flickers wanly from banks of computer screens. It smells of ozone and cheap industrial cleaner. Humming uneasily together, the electronics and air conditioning achieve a low and dissonant chord.

Bryce's UAV, launched by controllers overseas, is waiting to speed over the mountains towards a village believed to be hiding an important figure, a 'really big fish.' Intel has spoken.

Bryce takes control of the Predator. Joystick, throttle, readouts, radios, computers, GPS, satellites— he has all the technology he needs, but foremost is pure instinct. He streaks over sullen crags, swoops down long, ancient gorges with grace and ease, arcing up for the next sharp ridge, banking, dropping lower as the target nears, an insignificant enclave sleeping at the end of a sloping valley. The plane's amazing cameras reveal lazy smoke in the thin dawn light.

My dusk is your daybreak, my power your weakness, my knowledge your death. Where did that come from? Bryce wonders, readying to fire.

Headsets vibrate a crisp command. "Take out the center structures. That's affirmative."

Bryce sees rough, sand-colored buildings, sagging tents, tiny moving figures. *Women carrying water* his brain screeches, three, a detached voice counts down, *those can't be kids and goats*, two, *surely a trick of light*, one, a small flock of birds arises, veers abruptly, fire! Bryce launches the missiles, someone yells a triumphant "splash!" the village erupts in flaming dust, pixilated chaos, and Bryce pulls up and away, his temples pounding, impossibly hearing screams smelling bloodstench seeing shredded flesh tasting gritty bile feeling searing agony.

Bryce wants to believe he's only a force of nature, merciless yet dispassionate, only a great blue heron doing what he knows to do: fly, kill, fly.

But what, Bryce wonders, does a heron know of human error, of collateral damage?

"Awesome flying, Major!" mutters the captain. Her face has lost its ruddiness but her eyes maintain their steeled obedience.

Bryce nods, removes his fat, sweat-stained headsets, scribbles at his paperwork, creaks open the door of the olive and gray shipping container. Outside, he quickly jams on dark glasses against the accusing glare of the desert. He's assailed by an incongruous blend of smells: the stink of frying hamburgers and the earthy overtones of sage. Grease and sadness, he thinks, hold the fries.

Swallowing dust and bile, he swims through the heat and the sand towards the central trailer.

What does a heron know of nightmares?

Bryce clinks up the metal stairs, enters another sightless room, prepares to report.

And tonight another dream awaits, ready to close its dark-feathered walls around him.

Playing Doctor

Carolee at age 21, tricked by just one word, one name, into tumbling down the rabbit hole and thinking of herself at age six in Possum Hollow, Mississippi.

The name hopped right off the page. *Jiminey*. The playful kid next door. Sandy haired, kinda cute but too many freckles, shooting at cans with a homemade slingshot. Jiminey. Not Jim, Jimmy or Jim-boy. Jiminey. Like Pinocchio's little pal.

Only he wasn't named after the cricket. Another memory floated in, swirled around, clarified. His name. What was the story? Yeah, an older brother telling her Jiminey got his name because that's what his father cried out when he learned of the pregnancy. "Jiminey, not another one!" More likely, Carolee now thought, the word of exclamation had been much stronger, too shocking to use as a name. What were there, eight kids, nine, ten? Might as well have lived in a shoe.

She'd put one of her least favorite dolls down range, right there for Jiminey to shoot at with his twigs and rubber bands. Snapwham! The very first shot cracked that doll's cheek but good. The kid was as shocked as she was. Then he shrugged, a hint of pride.

The screen door creaked and slammed. Gramsie was coming out fast. Jiminey bolted in a puff of dust, trampling a trail of dandelions.

Gramsie was not happy. And an unhappy Gramsie was like a mean tornado uncurling rapidly inside a sadistic hurricane. Though Jiminey might have borne the brunt of this storm, Carolee thought it best to duck and run and scamper up one of her favorite trees, which happened to be a magnolia. Marvelous refuge and sweet smelling as a bonus. Gramsie hadn't taken to climbing up after her. Yet.

Below the tree, a whippoorwill, awakened by the ruckus, protested with a sleepy declaration of its name. *Caprimulgus vociferus.* Good thing the bird didn't try to sing in Latin.

However, back to Jiminey, the present day one. Carolee stared at the yearbook. The team pages. All bragging. All glory. All potential. Was this the same guy, now grown into a star college halfback? Fair hair, still sorta cute, only a touch stuck up. Too much Joe College and not enough little boy to recognize. But how many Jimineys could there be? She couldn't recall the kid's last name, something ordinary, a step up from Smith or Brown. This one, the jock, was an Alberts. Was that it?

But the chatty bio, the jock's listing: oh God, that seemed to settle it, washing her in guilt.

"Jiminey Alberts, junior starting halfback, always wanted to play quarterback, but lost the tip of a finger in his throwing hand when he was a boy. 'You should see what happens to my spirals,' he jokes. 'Big time kittywhompus!' Just the same, Alberts is happy to be setting school rushing records."

Lost a finger. Well, not exactly lost. If it was the same guy—and how it could not be?— Jiminey owed his spiral deficiency smack dab squarely to her, Carolee June Trimble.

Playing Doctor

As usual, the little doofus was out there among the hickories and pines getting his licks in with his gimcrack slingshot. Caveman sort of tool. But charming shmarming, disarming six-year-old Carolee knew about real tools and weapons. F'rinstance, she certainly knew her way around a knife. And that glarehot summer day she'd sneaked a gleaming knife out of the kitchen and taken it into the woods, ready to play doctor. Hickory dickory doc. Proper doctoring, not your nambypampy fumbling under a shirt or pretending a tin can was a stethoscope kind of doctoring. The real McCoy operating room kind of doc, scalpel and all. Well, knife and all. And a sharp knife indeed. Gramsie would have none other around.

Carolee also had pilfered the old clunky meat thermometer, assuming that would be a reasonable medical substitute.

At first Jiminey was all for it, this doctor game, carefully laying his precious slingshot in some friendly kudzu and then sprawling his twiggy little body among the black-eyed Susans.

"You gonna cure my ol' warts, doctor?" he giggled, flashing the gap between his crooked teeth.

"Be quiet and open wide. Gotta take your temperature." First she shook the meat thermometer as she'd seen Gramsie do with the real McCoy, and then she poked it into his gaping mouth. Maybe it would tell her if he was fish or fowl, pork or turkey.

Jiminey closed his eyes, tilting a face of freckles, dirt, sweat and innocence to the sky. A woodpecker above them hammered after grubs. Two white butterflies danced by, indifferent to all this OR drama.

Carolee saw no action on the meat-speckled dial, but what the heck, it was a game, so she withdrew the thermometer, held it up and said, gravely. "Oh, fever, my friend. Fever. Y'all have a temperature of...140 and rising for the stars."

He blinked up at her, only half-playing. "Is that bad?"

"Yep! Badder'n a black widder hiding in y'all's Halloween candy." She wasn't sure where that idea came from, but it sounded serious enough.

"So what ya gonna do, doc? Tickle me to make it better?" This kid wasn't stupid. Next he'd want to be the doctor, and heaven knows where he'd try to run his hands.

Carolee brandished the knife. "I'm going to amputate." She was proud of that word, picked up on some TV show. She repeated it with relish. "Amp—you—tate. You know, do some slicing, cut something off."

That got his attention and he sat up right smartly, staring at her. Carolee wasn't sure what she'd intended with the knife. Maybe giving Jiminey a thrill as she ran the flat of the blade up his arm. Maybe tracing a circle or two around his bellybutton, no blood, just a bit of dimpling. Maybe waving it hypnotically in front of his eyes till he fell asleep or wet his pants, whichever came first.

But for some reason, she thought, amputate, OK, why not? I can cut off one of his big old dirty fingernails real easy, and that would better fit the bill.

Playing Doctor

"I'm gonna remove your fever nail," she told him. "Easy stuff for a brain surgeon like me."

Jiminey winced. "I ain't got no nail in my brain, CJ, an even if I did, y'all ain't cutting on it."

"It's not in your brain, dummy. It's on your finger. And it won't hurt at bit. All you gotta do is lay back." Then, inspired: "Tell you what, I'll give you some knockout stuff, some good old Auntie Seezya."

A bit dubious, Jiminey settled down in the grass again, waving away a hovering dragonfly. "OK, but next it's my turn and I get to check y'all out for, for measles or rabies or something."

Carolee was already searching for her anesthetic. "Yeah, yeah." she told him. "Just lay there a sec." She debated using a stinky weed that smelled like dung, but decided that wasn't modern medicine. Not right for a lady doctor either. She spotted a wild rose, sliced it free with a deft swing of the knife and again crouched by to her patient.

"All right then, close y'all's eyes." She waved the rose close to Jiminey's nose. "Now sniff this."

"Hey, that ain't bad," he announced, sniffing heartily. "Smell's pretty good. What is it?"

"Auntie Seezya. Auntie Septic. One of them aunts. Shut up and go to sleep. You gotta pass out before I can do any cutting." She moved the rose in front of his face again. Jiminey gave an appreciative sigh then snorted a loud snore. The kid was playing his part.

Carolee hefted the knife, lifted Jiminey's right hand and looked for the best fingernail to pare. His index finger sported a truly vile protrusion. It was long, jagged, grimed with red clay and what might or might not have been mustard. She didn't want to dwell on the source. She wiped the sweat out of her eyes with the back of her hand, then proudly using all the poise she'd seen on television, she twirled the knife around this bit of grossness and moved in for the cut.

Whoever said timing is everything sure said a mouthful. Who'd have guessed, for instance, at that exact knife-arcing moment some dumb polecat, not knowing day from night, would rumble out of a hollow log and rustle though a pile of dried-up ferns.

Jiminey twitched at the sound, Carolee started at the sudden flash of black and white, and the knife, its eye on the prize, neatly severed the top of Jiminey's finger. One good thing: that ugly old fingernail was also a goner.

Serenity. Immobility. One thousand one, one thousand two. Then a scream that stopped all the cicada chatter plumb cold. Bright blood in the air. Jiminey staring aghast at his mutilated hand. One pissed-off skunk, old *Mephitis mephitis* herself, stamping her foot and hissing. Carolee thinking wow, this ain't good, neither the quality of the surgery nor the angry stinkbomb raising her tail and looking about to fire.

Jiminey squealed like a piglet. "You kilt me!" he wailed. His eyes rolled back and he fainted. The skunk, thinking better of it, dropped tail, shrugged and waddled off. The cicadas went back to their busy jawing.

As Carolee was trying to make some kind of bandage out of her grimy handkerchief, she heard the most dreaded sound of all, a stretched-out squeal and a hard rickety bam. Gramsie! What big ears she had. Well, even if the whirlwind was a-coming, even if Carolee's legs were telling her to hightail it and fast, she couldn't desert her patient.

She was wrapping the bloodied handkerchief over Jiminey's finger when Gramsie burst into the clearing. "What y'all done now, CJ?" she barked. "Christ ahmighty! I'm raising a serial killer!"

Anger took second place to doing the right thing. Gramsie shoved Carolee aside, quickly assessed the problem, tightened the makeshift bandage, picked Jiminey up like he was a sack of yams and thundered back toward the house. Her ominous "I'll deal with y'all later, CJ!" rumbled back through the trees.

At that moment no one thought about the top of Jiminey's finger, lying there like a fat red June bug. Later, when they came looking for it, it had gone, maybe filched by a sharp-eyed jay. Or maybe sneaked away by that darn polecat, aiming for revenge for all the commotion. So there could be no miracle of stitching it back on.

Meantime, Carolee had treed herself. Where else? She went higher than usual up into her favorite magnolia and perched up there panting and sweating. As she inhaled the melancholy sweetness, she wondered which might come first, the wrath of the Almighty or the fury of Gramsie. She sure knew which would be more severe.

But Gramsie, when she came looking for Carolee, stood down below shaking her head and was surprisingly mild. "Awright, he'll live. That's the main thing. But he ain't gonna be sticking that finger up his nose anytime soon."

She peered into the tree. "What was y'all trying to do, CJ? Circumcision?"

"Circumsister? Don't know what that is, Gramsie."

"Well, then, never you mind for now. You wasn't aiming to chop off his hand, was you?

"No, ma'am. Just cut off a big old fingernail. We was playing doctor, that's all. Darn polecat made him jump and the knife got him."

Gramsie snorted and passed wind, one of her favorite pastimes. Carolee reckoned Gramsie might well have been a polecat in some other life.

"Well, then," said Gramsie, remarkably amiably. "C'mon down. They taken Jiminey to the doctor for stitching, so you and me might as well have a slice of pecan pie."

Carolee thought about it for a moment. Her grandmother wasn't given to being devious. For some reason she wasn't hopping mad like you'd have expected. And pecan pie was the lure of all lures. So she began to descend, curling and uncurling round the branches like a maypole streamer unwinding. Then a hesitation, just out of Gramsie's reach.

"You ain't agonna clobber me?"

"Naw, CJ. This is one bit of nonsense I sure do understand."

Carolee dropped to the soft ground. "You do?"

They started back to the house. "Y'all probably can't comprehend the fact that I was a girl once myself. Not that many centuries back either. So I'm mighty familiar

Playing Doctor

with playing doctor. Oh, yes! And familiar with them little types of accidents too."

Carolee swatted at a lazy wasp. "You cut off some boy's ear or something?"

Gramsie hooted and farted, a noisy combination which seemed to satisfy her no end.

"Back then a girl wouldn't be no doctor. We was always the patients. But when Ozzie Hicks tried to feel...well, let's say he went a little too far. And I kneed that sneaky sonofagun right in the balls, 'scuse my French, CJ. He was in a world of hurt for a long time."

"You kicked a kid in his private parts?"

"More or less, yes."

"Wow!"

"Kneejerk reaction, I guess, speaking in the truest sense. But between you and me and that old wheelbarrow, mighty, mighty satisfying."

That particular slice of pecan pie was mighty satisfying too, Carolee remembered. But that was her last summer living with Gramsie, who upped and died that fall without asking a by your leave.

It wasn't fair. Two years back, Carolee's parents had gone to heaven in one fell swoop collision with a furniture truck. Gramsie dropped decades too soon with a massive stroke. Out of the blue Carolee found herself living with Aunt Elsie and Uncle Carter over in Louisiana, fearful they might be taken next.

She had plenty to think about, and Slidell was a far enough piece from Possum Hollow that little Jiminey was soon forgotten. His fingertip too.

Until now. What, fifteen or sixteen years later, and there's this guy staring back from the Ole Miss Yearbook. God, she'd screwed up or at least changed his big-time football plans. What else had that skunktriggered slice done? Carolee imagined that if Jiminey had any thoughts of being a concert pianist or some other kind of fingerlickin, fingerpickin musician, those dreams might be deader than a nest of fire ants doused with a kettle of scalding water.

Well, guilt only goes so far, she thought, slamming the yearbook closed. He's had plenty of years to adjust and reset his life, and I guess he's doing pretty fine, star halfback and all, thank you very much. Kinda weird for me to be at Ole Miss all this time and never run into him. Of course she was one of the few oddballs who didn't follow the football stuff, not one of those giggly coeds with tongues hanging out, arms eager to latch on to those BMOCs in their cute old rebel sweatshirts and their hotshot airs.

Carolee had never thought to make it to college, much less to Old Miss. But first there was the money Gramsie had secretly squirreled away for her little CJ. And then came the scholarships, earned fair and square. A tomboy with a brain. That's what Uncle Carter had called her. She'd cleaned up her act, improved her language—well mostly—and even was thinking seriously about graduate school.

So the fingershort jock went one way and the brainy tomboy another and never the twain shall meet. At least that's what Carolee thought as she prepared to wrap up her final quarter.

Playing Doctor

Well, it never rains but it shits, Gramsie used to say, rarely that sensitive to young ears and minds. Just three days after confronting her bloody past in the yearbook, Carolee reluctantly agreed to go with her friend Julie to a party at a house on Frat Row and within minutes came smack face to face with one Jiminey Alberts.

Figures, she thought, trying not to look too shifty-eyed.

Another friend of Julie's was screaming introductions over the hubbub. "An' this is Carolee Trimble, one of those hotshot biology majors."

"Tttrimble?" he mused, if that's what you can do in the racket of a frat party. "I think there was some Ttrimbles back where I lived as a kkkid. Where y'all from?"

Oh, God, a stutter. Was that another result of her doctoring? Jeesh, now he couldn't be a opera star either. Not even a TV announcer.

"I live over in Slidell," Carolee told him, having to lean in closer than she wanted, though she noticed he smelled nice. Lightly tropical and deliciously creamy. Beat the fraternity smell of sweat, testosterone, hops and fried chicken by a long shot.

"Yeh, next dddoor in Possum Hollow, that's where they were. Hardscrabble ppatch a little north of Hattiesburg." The freckles had smoothed out beautifully, and the eyes were, damn, kinda sexy. The long lashes really did it.

"My only relatives are in Louisiana," she said, truthful at least about the present day.

"CJ, that was her nn-name!" Jiminey exclaimed. " CJ! I hadn't remembered that in a why-why-while. I wonder—"

The party surged and swirled around them and Carolee was swept one way, Jiminey, another. She was off the hook. Or so she thought.

But maybe Gramsie was pulling the strings from heaven, because some time later, after Carolee had escaped to a relatively quiet back porch and was sitting on a wicker loveseat, hoping to see fireflies, and waiting for Julie so they could leave, here came that stutter at her ear.

"Fiff if found you!" He sat down uninvited. "Carolee, right?"

"Yep." Darn, was that a firefly over there? Maybe *Lampyris noctiluca* or *Photinus pyralis*?

"You sure ssstand out."

"Why's that?" She turned to him.

"Well, it don't lllook like you're the party type." He had a kind smile.

"I'm not. Just came to please a friend."

"Me neither," he declared. "The papa party type. Bbbut I got ob, obligations. Team needs me to sshow show up."

"Is football your life?" she found herself asking and immediately hearing Gramsie's voice. *OK, y'all could be in for it now, CJ!*

"Ga gag gosh, no." He really was a very earnest guy. All at once Carolee saw little Jiminey hiding shyly right below the surface.

He held up—ohmygod—his hand, the hand, and studied it. "I wanted to be a doctor," he said. "A bbbrain sssurgeon. But I had this accident when I was a kkkkid, so..."

The finger rose into full view. It wasn't at all startling, an ordinary digit simply missing everything above the top joint. She couldn't help staring, fascinated beyond her hidden knowledge and discomfort. And beyond a fresh attack of guilt. *A doctor, CJ.!* Gramsie tittered. *Who'da thunk?*

Carolee forced herself to keep looking. A pink fold of skin neatly capped the finger, and everything seemed quite normal. Well, except...

Jiminey didn't reveal the least trace of anger or self-pity. "I'm still thinking of gggoing to med school," he told her. "Bbbut I might aim fffor psychiatry. Lot easier. I can cut into mminds without needing any fuff fingers."

She was amazed how he had no trouble with the bigger words, only the ordinary ones. Amazed, too, at how affable and likeable he was. *Easy, now, CJ*, Gramsie whispered with a low chuckle.

He went on. "And this annoying ssspeech thing won't mmmatter. A shrink only sits and lllistens, right? Bbbut enough about my plans. What about yu you?"

The guy's blue eyes were dazzling. He was down-to-earth. He was thoughtful. He was intelligent. All that in a jock? Boy, was she stereotyping.

His subtle cologne and his pure physical warmth radiated lazily over her. The air on the porch carried a promise of impending rain. Out in the dark somewhere, the crickets, most likely *Gryllinae: gryllidae* she thought, had ceased their own stuttering, were hunkering down.

Goodness me, she thought. Jiminey and the crickets. One hell of a group, a hit for sure.

"Well, wwwhat about you?" he repeated.

So, where to start on her resume? Truth, half-truth, convenient omissions or outright lies? In any case, keep it simple, she thought. But instead she startled herself and, from his reaction, Jiminey.

"I don't go out with football players!" She announced. Where did that come from? He hadn't even asked.

But she knew he would ask. And worse, she knew she would say yes. The only unanswered question, really, was if and when she'd spill the beans, the okra, the black-eyed peas, the whole kettle of catfish about her significant role in shaping his life. With a knife. Carolee June Trimble, his personal carver.

Meantime, Gramsie in heaven, restless, muttered and farted. Or was that distant thunder?

So of course they began going out, and things went pretty well considering the secret nimbus which hovered over her like a turkey vulture, *Cathartes aura*. She thought she surely had to tell him, but the timing had to be just right. It helped that the subject hadn't come up again. *Just y'all wait,* Gramsie snorted.

They discovered they both liked Faulkner and took to strolling across the campus and through Bailey Woods to the grounds of Rowan Oak, where the great author had lived. Lingering on the edge of the woods, they liked the way the timeless, white high-columned building peeked back through the trees.

"I heard a great story from one of my English profs," said Carolee as they leaned against a huge spreading oak, not touching, but comfortably close. "When he was just a freshman at Vanderbilt, he came down to Oxford for a looksee. Probly called it slumming. Anyway, he found himself over this way, and as naïve as a newt, he wandered right up to Faulkner's house and knocked on the door."

Jiminey chuckled "Wow! I was a dddumbass kid, but nnever that fffoolish."

Carolee laughed with him. The oak was rough but still felt supple and supportive beneath her shoulder blades. "Me too. But the amazing thing is that good ole Bill Faulkner himself opened the door. He was wearing a tatty plaid shirt and dirty red suspenders, with a pipe perched in his mouth. And when he saw this teenager standing there, would you believe Faulkner went ahead and opened the screen door too, stepped out onto that little porch and made the kid right welcome, chatted with him for some time."

"Wwwhat would you ever find to say to sssomeone like Faulkner?"

"Me, I'd have been tongue-tied. I guess they talked a bit about this and that. And then the stupid kid right about put his foot in it by asking, 'What's the point of studying lit anyway?' And Faulkner looks him right in the eye, lets out a big puff of smoke and says, 'Read my books. If they don't answer your question, nothing will.' Not big on modesty, was our old Bill."

"That's great! I can almost sssee them on the ppporch right now." Jiminey sighed with pleasure.

Carolee turned her gaze from the magic of Rowan Oaks and looked at Jiminey. Two tiny drops of sweat twinkled on his forehead. He'd missed shaving a little island of sandy hair under his lips. A small black ant ran in crazy circles near his collar. Jiminey brought his hand up to scratch his neck. And, suddenly, there was that durn finger, breaking the mood.

Their shared attraction was evident from the getgo, and the romantic side blossomed very quickly. But the purely physical proceeded slowly, which for some reason pleased and thoroughly satisfied her. The other college guys she'd dated always seemed to have but one goal in mind. *Yep, and sometimes they scored, didn't they?* clucked Gramsie.

Jiminey didn't push, didn't grope, was affectionate, was always relaxed. He liked to hold her hand, and he kissed her with a rare combination of intensity and sweetness. Her own considerable passion was happily in thrall to a giddy sense of belonging and rightness. There was no rush. She was delighted to realize they were behaving like childhood sweethearts, lighthearted and innocent.

Football was not her thing, but once in a while she perched nervously in the bright, sultry raucousness of Vaught-Hemingway while Jiminey strutted his stuff on the field. Stuttered his stuff, she thought, far too unkindly. Especially since she'd noticed that the more relaxed they were with each other, the less he stuttered in her presence. Small blessings, she felt, then chided

Playing Doctor

herself. In a way she needed the stutter and the odd-topped finger to remind her she had something to expiate.

Jiminey sure was a scrambler. Fast, agile, he could dodge, twist, pivot, sprint and rack up the yards, and the thunderous Rebels fans loved him. Maybe those spirals he'd wanted to throw didn't matter. As least she hoped not.

Whether celebrations or wakes, the post-game parties held little interest, and Carolee and Jiminey would duck out as quickly as they could. They liked to saunter down to the historic district and forgo the nightspots for the relative quiet in the leafy heart of the courthouse square. Always the trees, she thought. Right from our kiddiehood.

"When I was a little girl, I loved to climb trees," she found herself telling him. That seemed safe enough to mention. Nearby a banjo plinked tentatively then burst into a cascade of tinkled merriment. The night air was deliciously heavy with the fragrance of late-season gardenias.

"And, I loved to run around barefoot." *Hey, CJ, nudged Gramsie, y'all might be opening a can o' worms here.*

"Bbet you were a tomboy," he said.

"Yep." Leave it at that, she told herself. Gramsie sniggered again: *Big fat, fingersized worms.*

"Me too," Jiminey said. "The barefoot type, I mean. Ppossum Hollow was the ppperfect place for it. Mostly woods, really. What it's like over in your part of Lll Louisiana?"

"Oh, you know. Swamps, rivers, bayous. Em, herons, gators, that sort of stuff. Hey, you wanta go barefoot right this minute?" She slipped off her sandals.

He bent to untie his sneakers. "Tell me about your ppparents. What are they like?" Oh oh, time to tiptoe through the swamps of truth and not-truth, barefoot and all.

"They died when I was very young. I was raised by my Grandmother and later by an Aunt and Uncle."

"Huh. That reminds me of—what was—oh, yeah, that little girl, name of, eh, CJ. Yeah, it was CJ! She was a nnnay, neighbor kid, lived with her grandmother. We pupplayed together a lot."

"Hey, the grass feels great, doesn't it?" She splayed her toes. Ten perfect digits.

He wasn't distracted. "I never told you how I lost my fffingertip, did I?"

"An accident, you said." *Hey, don't keep it going,* Gramsie whispered. *You better divert this real quick. Scream, faint, throw up, or better yet climb a tree, and fast!*

"Well, it's a little fffuzzy. I was only five or sssix. But CJ and me were out in the woods playing doctor..." He laughed. "Sss-stupid, huh?"

"Well, no, not necessarily, I guess lots of kids..." She trailed off. *Some diversion!* scoffed Gramsie.

"I musta been hoping to touch her bbubbellybutton or something. You know how little boys are."

Big ones too warned Gramsie. *Past and present, this Jiminey's more than he seems.*

Carolee, despite herself—and despite Gramsie—was very curious about her CJ days. "So, what was whatshername, CK, like?"

"CJ. Well, she was real cute. But a little ffffull of herself."

"What do you mean 'full of herself?" It came out a bit strong. Oops, don't get defensive.

"She was smart and she knew it. Sssweet and tough both, I guess. I kinda had a cccrush on her. If you can have a cccrush when you're that young."

"I think you can. Have a crush" A pause. In for a penny. "Ever want to kiss her?"

Jiminey thought about it. "Maybe I did. I dunno. But I'd a gotten into big tttrouble."

"Trouble?"

"CJ lived with this demon grandma. If you did something wrong, that old lady always knew it and came ssshooting into the woods like a bat out of hehehell. I'd have tried a kiss and she fffound out, she'da stuck my lllips together with ssssuperglue." He smiled. "Oh, another thing I'll never forget: that grandmother bbbackfired like a pickup too!"

They both laughed. That was Gramsie all right: *Flatulare iconoclastis.*

Side by side, they scuffed through the grass. A welcome breeze danced into the square, moving to fragments of distant Dixieland. Carolee thought OK, if he tells the story now, we won't have to deal with it again. He doesn't have the foggiest idea he's talking to the demon's grandkid. I'll be off the hook, no true confessions, no mea culpas required.

"So, the accident?" she prompted, feeling Gramsie right at her ear. *Y'all playing with fire now, CJ.*

Jiminey scratched his ear. "Oh, yeah. Well, I seem to remember that CJ bbbrought out a bbbunch of tools. She didn't ever do things halfway. She had this bbbig knife and I guess was gggonna tickle me with it or something. But I dunno, somehow the knife jumped, and...slicey dicey. I was pppretty much out of it after that, don't remember much mum more."

"Slicey dicey?" What had Jiminey thought it was, a Vegematic commercial?

"Pretty messy I heard. They couldn't find the...you know, top of my fffinger. They told me a wild pig or a turkey or something had probly ggggobbled it up." He laughed. "Only fffair, considering what we all chow down at Thanksgiving."

"That's mighty open-minded of you, Jiminey."

"Yeah, well. So for a time I was lllost to the world. They stitched me up, I guess, and eventually I lllearned to live with this."

He waved his hand like a baton, perfectly in time to the steady low drumbeat coming from a nightclub across the square. Carolee's stared at the injured finger, a hypnotic summons from years back. Might as well round this out, she thought.

"So what happened to the girl? They throw her in jail?"

"Naw. But I'll bbet that grandma of hers gave her a good licking."

"Gosh, I hope so!" *Darn right!* chortled Gramsie. *You sure licked the plate clean after that big piece of pecan pie!*

Carolee continued: "Despite everything, did you stay friends?"

"I would have. But I didn't see her mmmuch after it happened, then she mmmoved away. Jackson or Tupelo or someplace. Too bad. I lilliked her."

"Even after she carved you up?

"It wasn't CJ's fffault. Just an accident."

That's your cue, thought Carolee. Couldn't be better. He doesn't blame you. Fess up, see what happens. *Are you kidding?* Gramsie hooted, *It's all nostalgia now, but see what happens when he learns you're his Dr. Frankenstein.*

"I didn't make a monster," Carolee murmured aloud.

"What?" asked Jiminey.

"I said you're very generous."

"Naw, not rrreally," he said, smiling shyly. "Y'know, you remind me a little of sssis-CJ. More than a little. Could be that's why I like you so much."

"Gonna be a full moon, you suppose?" *Pert limp distraction, that!* Carolee stared at the sky and tried to will herself into looking less like that darn little CJ.

Jiminey stood very close. "Sssay, what about if we play dddoctor one of these days? Sssoon. You and me."

Startled, she almost jumped. This wasn't her kind of déjà vu. "Yikes!" she babbled. "I'm not into knives. I can hardly handle my dissections. I've been afraid of knives since I was a kid." *Since y'all cut his finger off, ain't that it?* Gramsie never let up.

He put his arm around her. "Nnno knives, silly. I was just trying to use a mmeta-mmetaphor. You know, kinda like Faulkner?"

"Jeezus, Jiminey. Faulkner, metaphors, knives. Y'all want to sleep with me, why don't you just say so?"

He stared at her, his mouth open. Then he smiled. God, was he cute. Then and now.

"I was trying to be cool and ease into it," he said softly. "But hell, yes. Ain't it about time, Carolee? You know I'm crazy about you."

Shocked silence. They both had noticed. No stutter at all. Finally she started to speak.

"Jimi—" He put his damaged finger on her lips and cut her off.

"That's right. That's what you should call me. Jimmy or maybe even Jim. I'm grown up now. Might even become James when I get that MD."

Carolee tried them all out. "Jimmy. Jim. James. Yes, maybe it's about time." *Y'all sure about this, CJ?* Gramsie's sarcasm had vanished. This was a tone of gentle concern.

"I'm sure."

They sat on the soft edge of the bed in the darkened room, holding each other, looking out. The window was wide open. Busy crickets held late evening conversations between bursts of a sprinkler. The moon threw pewter over the trees. The rich perfumes of the night curled sensuously round them, jasmine, spider lilies, ancient loam, damp leaves, and—she had to laugh—a faint and friendly scent of skunk.

Playing Doctor

Then she was lying in bed with her star halfback Jiminey Jimmy Jim James Alberts, *Smartandcuteus semidigitus*, enthralled to be in the arms of her past, her present and, who knew, maybe her future. She lifted his hand and kissed his index finger.

"So let's play doctor," she said. "Our own special way." She gently moved his finger and let its incredible smoothness brush over her firm nipple. Once. Twice. Electric. Sublime. That was all the guiding he needed.

Later, she thought how the smallest moments can substantially change a life. But not just his life, she was a bit startled to realize. Without the accident, she'd have had no lingering guilt, no jolt of memory. She might never have made this reconnection.

She kissed his finger again. Half asleep, he sighed something, smiled, and closed his eyes.

But, do I tell him? Now? Tomorrow? Ever? Does he need to know? Would he see me differently? Would it change anything? Change everything?

She lay there, thinking drowsily. The warm fall night, redolent of decay and abundance, settled in around them.

For once, Gramsie had nothing to say.

Late

Adam is running late for his own funeral.

The hearse rolls down the country lane at a somber speed, backfiring. Adam has to laugh, since his last months alive had been punctuated—*nice word*, he thinks—with episodes of flatulence.

If I'd had to deal only with that, I wouldn't have minded, embarrassing as it was. Then again, isn't dying itself embarrassing?

As the hearse burps along, Adam stops to peer into a bird's nest on an upper branch of a tall maple. The fuzzy, hungry chicks don't seem aware of him. He smiles at their downy innocence then flies off again.

Flies? Well, he isn't sure that flying is what he's actually doing. He thinks it's wonderful, whatever it is. *Soaring? Levitating? Just being? Certainly just being.*

And now, suddenly, Adam is at ground level, smelling late-blooming lilacs, reveling in the honeyed musk of early roses.

Pity to die in summer. Well, pity to die at all. Redwing blackbirds whistle-screech, and he's instantly over the hedges to hover by the bulrush marsh, watching the swaying scarlet and black. No, not just watching. Bobbing, calling out desire. He feels strangely happy.

Why this joy? Why all this joy? Oh, but I'm late for something. I'm late.

He remembers the white rabbit from Alice in Wonderland and then realizes he *is* the white rabbit at that moment. *Hmm. Do moments still exist for me?* He doesn't remember being at all philosophical in life. After all he was a...*what was I anyway? Car salesman? No. Computer tech? Don't think so. Teacher? Can't remember.* He knows it didn't matter in the least. Not then. Not now.

I'm late, I'm late, for a most important date. He reaches back with an invisible hand to see if he's grown a cottontail, and there it is. Or is it? He laughs, and immediately returns to floating over the lane. *Floating. Is that it?* He watches the hearse round the last curve, slow down, backfire once more, and turn onto the narrow dirt trail to the cemetery. To his gravesite.

My gravesite. Some rabbit hole <u>that</u> is! Surely that can't be Wonderland. No time to stop or hesitate. I'm late...

He perches—*am I perching, sailing, drifting?*— in the rumpled fork of an ancient oak and watches pallbearers, sweating in black suits, unload the hearse. The casket slides easily onto their shoulders. It is shiny, sleek, a gorgeous mahogany. *Someone's getting the best treatment. Oh. That's funny. That someone is me. Was me.*

A sizeable crowd stands quietly, waiting for the casket to be placed onto a graveside stand. *Is this mob here for me?*

Adam, a butterfly, flutters over one of the big floral wreaths, alights on a laurel leaf.

I never was the life of the party. And here I am, the life of the party. Sort of. He opens and shuts his brilliant batik wings, soft as goodbye kisses.

Late

Someone speaks, people sit down on folding chairs, and the service begins.

Adam listens with dreamstate nonchalance. He is a sunbeam, thistledown gliding in the air, a white gardenia petal fallen on the bier. Incantations, lamentations, truths—some stretched—fictions—some enchanting— memories—some very inaccurate: all wash over him, warm and cool, meaningful and meaningless.

Everyone stands. Music begins. *My God, who chose 'Amazing Grace'? I'd have picked...* But he can think of no other tune besides something about a yellow submarine, and he isn't sure that would fit. So he joins in and belts out 'Amazing Grace', somehow knowing all the lyrics, the best voice in the cemetery, rising above the whole congregation, operatic, soul-stunning. Unheard.

Eulogies over, music fading, Adam, an ant, crawls to the edge of the waiting grave. It is dark and moist, murmuring of earthworms. The casket descends toward him, a huge ship launched. It slides close by—past, present, and future slipping together down the deep chasm.

Adam tries to sense himself inside the coffin, but he isn't there.

He's here, a forgotten daisy in the dirt.

He's here, blade of grass bending gravewards from sorrow or from politeness.

He is there, a long-stemmed rose ready for tossing, for dying.

And he's there, a teardrop creasing a cheek.

Loitering, That's what I'm doing. Loitering. Flying, floating, soaring, hovering, levitating, yes—but also loitering. Whatever's next, I'm late, I'm late.

There is the tiniest of thuds. The earth sighs. The casket has arrived. *I'm late, I'm late. Or, perhaps I'm right on time.*

As the funeral party drives out along the cemetery trail—disbelief, relief, grief, and all the other unrealities of death rising in the dust and sunbeams—an eagle strokes the air above, commanding; a tiny sapling pokes up through the nearby forest floor, hopeful; a white rabbit zigzags into the clovered fields, curious...

...and vanishes as though never there.

Spoons

Each piece of flatware had its place. The drawer was meticulously divided for logic, utility and harmony.

Dinner forks commanded the left slot. Next, salad forks.

Then—continuing to the right—knives, soupspoons, teaspoons and, in the penultimate place, a special slot for those tiny spoons so necessary for carefully eating soft boiled eggs. (Two minutes, 35 seconds, perfectly timed.)

To the right of these small spoons: a second special slot for their cousins, the everyday demitasse spoons, rugged but demure, nicely reminiscent of the kitchen playsets of childhood.

Everything nested companionably. All tines and scooping edges faced up. All handles faced south. The drawer whispered open and shut on delicate glides. Minding its manners.

A separate drawer held selected utensils, each also with its appropriate location. The liner slots had been custom-made after thoughtful consideration of every possible need. Tongs there, meat carving set here, thermometers here, skewers there. Spatulas, slotted servers and serving forks, there, there and there.

Everything with a place. Everything *in* its place.

The cupboards were laid out strategically to provide the most accessible spots for: dinner plates (12), salad plates (12) bowls (8), cups (8), saucers (8), glasses (12, but there were an additional 2 childhood memento glasses holding emeritus places near the others). Each stack of dishes was precisely-aligned, inspection ready, each glass inverted and squared away.

Norma and Molly had washed and dried the supper dishes together for 27 years, every single year they'd lived together.

Allowing for the occasional meal out, their annual vacation, illness and so on, the nightly shared ritual came to something like 8,721 evenings of washing and drying.

Factoring out cleaning up after breakfasts and lunches, those nightly sacraments had required about 4,210 ounces of detergent, 424 scrub pads, 319 dishcloths and 297 dishtowels, those last handmade, the worn ones scrupulously recycled as household rags or as quilting scraps. They wore out 54 aprons and 12 kitchen mats.

They changed the lights bulb over the sink just 17 times and required plumbers only twice.

They went for 12 years straight without breaking a cup, glass or plate, then, after a minor crockery accident during that brief period when their relationship wobbled ever so slightly, they settled back in and broke nothing for another 15 years. And still counting.

There was never a question of acquiring a dishwasher. Neither of their large families had owned a dishwasher. In both families it was expected that all children between roughly eight and thirteen would participate in cleaning up after the evening meal. One child would wash and the other would dry. Alternating

Spoons

who did what was permitted. Tradeoffs were allowed by prior approval if there was a good reason such as special homework, a major test upcoming or an evening piano recital. Gender was irrelevant, though the boys spent a great deal of time trying figure out ways to avoid the chores entirely.

Apart from both growing up with this family norm, when Molly and Norma moved in together, they soon rediscovered the sociability of working side by side, the pleasure of transforming soiled dishes, glasses and utensils into clean, glistening, satisfying objects, the comfort of returning everything to a predictable resting place. They loved the reassuring warmth of the water, the lemony scent of the detergent, the balanced heft of their everyday china and well-chosen flatware, the sense of order restored in drawers and cupboards.

They loved the cups of rosehip tea they allowed themselves after putting everything away, closing doors, disinfecting counters, hanging up towels and cloths and aprons. In 27 years, they had enjoyed approximately 816 gallons of rosehip tea, perhaps a little less if you allow for occasional forays into apricot, mint or ginger and one season of a Darjeeling-Assam blend, proven eventually to be too stimulating for imbibing at night.

This particular December evening, they had finished a supper of satsuma and walnut salad, roast rosemary chicken with herbed red potatoes and Norma's own mocha crème brulee for two.

The kitchen was pleasantly warm, feeling even cozier each time the pane-rattling winds fussed outside. The kettle was on to boil, the two cups and two matching saucers were standing ready for the sacramental tea.

The dishes were all washed, dried and tucked in for the night. Molly and Norma were finishing the silverware (as Molly always insisted on calling the flatware, though there wasn't a drop of precious metal in the lot). Norma used a scrub pad to remove a recalcitrant piece of potato from a final knife. Molly nestled spoons, admiring the fit, enjoying the soft clink of togetherness.

Norma handed Molly the knife. Molly dried it and gently placed it on top of its fellows, made a small adjustment to an errant handle, slid the drawer shut.

The grandfather clock chimed eight. The kettle whistled. They took off their aprons, hung them on their respective hooks in the pantry, quietly closed the pantry door, turned to each other.

As adults, they'd added something to their nightly ritual. Children dishwashing would never have thought of doing it. Of if anyone had tried it back then, there would have been giggling, wriggling, poking, and scampering away.

But now, as every night, Molly and Norma concluded their washing up with a hug—just one of the many small routines forming the mosaic that is love.

Had they been counting, they might have noticed that this hug—including all the other hugs in their relationship—this hug took them to a very nice-sounding figure: it was hug number 42,242.

Beneath

Andrew Fullerton lived in his imagination.

Since his childhood, it had provided refuge and adventure. Now that he was an artist, his imagination often seemed his nemesis.

Andrew seduced the canvas with olive and lapis lazuli. His palette knife ravaged rising and plunging textures with carmine and umber. His brushes darted, danced.

The undercoat disappeared, pigment and images ascended. A curving river sang, wet clouds embraced shy morning skies with whiffs of rain and yearning. Cottonwoods and willows swayed, whispering of hidden birds, of mystery.

Soon the osprey would rise over the water, faint blood on her trailing talons.

Layers of paint, layers of meaning.

Mozart filled the room, surged through Andrew's hand. Andrew followed each strand of harmony. Distinguished every instrument. Heard loose cufflinks in counter-rhythm against the conductor's starched sleeves.

Andrew's studio, a cacophony of paints and solvents, drop cloths and detritus, occupied the upper floor of an old mock Tudor in Boise's North End. Enlarged dormers framed mature elms. Twisting pines yielded to daredevil nuthatches. A tall end window held ochre foothills and distant promises. Oversized skylights cast sumptuous light.

This was his aerie, his keep. No one, not even Claire when she'd been with him, came up without invitation. Invitations were rare.

The Fullertons had moved from Colorado to join the Boise State faculty. People liked them. Andrew grew entertainingly eccentric as he flexed his painting talents. Claire brought passion into teaching early childhood education. They were a striking pair, he with a dancing limp, wild sandy hair and highlander stockiness, and she cooling rooms with her tall patrician darkness, heating them with her tantalizing austerity. They had no children, so they were available for competitive academic socializing, a pair of bright salmon jostling upstream.

Then came some sort of inheritance or insurance money or lottery winnings—Boise's gossipmongers were stymied—and the Fullertons bought the old Ridenbaugh House. They became much less of a public couple. Claire left the university to teach autistic children, and Andrew disappeared into his fulltime studio.

The art department chair, Tom Kaiser, whose abstract brown swirls were the constant delight of Boise, didn't mourn Andrew's defection. Less competition in the ranks. And then there was Claire, these days out and about by her gorgeous self while Andrew painted. Kaiser had an eye for beauty, a taste for the exotic. Claire seemed... vulnerable.

Andrew was prolific. But his work unnerved. He fit no one style or school. His paintings were marked by something no one could quite finger. Many viewers felt

Beneath

unease, but couldn't explain it. Others were drawn in but quickly squirmed in retreat.

Former colleagues were unflattering. "His stuff's proficient," said Kim Carter. "If off-putting."

Hector Ortiz sharpened a pencil. "And complex. But what does it mean?""

"Complexity alone doesn't mean anything." said Sheldon Merck. He thought he'd use that line in a lecture. Merck's acrylics were sentimental treatments of bygone Idaho. The public adored them.

A gallery-goer confronted Andrew. Onion breath, cilantro-flecked teeth.

"So what are you? Realist? Expressionist? What kind of 'ist' are you?"

Andrew didn't hesitate. "I'm a Fullertonist." The term quickly got around. It did nothing to endear him to the art community.

If his public ego seemed ferocious, privately Andrew knew doubt. He'd grown up with doubt. Doubt, guilt and death.

His childhood was rife with troubles and tragedy. Because of his congenital limp, because of his abundance of freckles and ungovernable hair, and especially because of his abilities, Andrew was mocked by other kids. They didn't understand different. They feared it. They didn't understand brilliance. They loathed it. He found it discomfiting that people still felt this way.

He stirred solvent, savoring the piney odors, appreciating the hypnotic swirl. He thought about the rivers he loved. The Boise, the Snake. The Colorado.

When Andrew was eight, his father died in a rafting accident. James Fullerton was only 32, brilliant, forever testing the limits. In dreams, Andrew flailed beneath the churning waters of the Colorado, lungs exploding, grasping for his father's hand, trying to save him.

James' death shattered Andrew's always-fragile mother, Susan. She sought solace in remarriage. Gregory Holt was a wealthy rancher, a handsome, vigorous man.

But Holt's perpetual grin hid a cruel nature. Andrew was derided, degraded. He was punished for the smallest infractions and, most of all, for his bookishness and his artistic leanings. Holt set young Andrew to shoveling mule shit on frigid mornings, locked him in rat-ridden woodsheds, thrashed the boy with bridles, their terrifying bits still attached. Andrew's memory snapped shut around other dark moments.

Susan, lost, no defender for her son, endured her own abuse. She retreated into a state of socialite torpor, hosting lavish parties while shrouding psychic bruises under expensive outfits and trying to temper everything with prescription drugs. She died of an overdose soon after Andrew escaped to college. He was certain it was suicide. He forever lamented their estrangement.

The only good thing arising from this past was the inheritance which came to Andrew after Greg Holt was kicked to death by a terrified bronco. *Blood money*, Andrew thought. But he took it, seeing his future open like the vast expanses of a Bierstadt landscape.

Freed, he pushed his skills in remarkable ways. Color, light, texture jumped under his brush, his knife, his hand. He invented new techniques to combine realism and ambiguity. But it wasn't enough.

He came up against a wall. Public acceptance was lukewarm, critical understanding lacking. Andrew couldn't break through.

He had one professional ally, the owner of the Zwiller Gallery in downtown Boise. Ned Zwiller was an edgy little man whose standup hair reminded Andrew of a much-tormented sable brush. Zwiller felt unsettled by Andrew's work, but he liked having a genius in his gallery,

Zwiller peered closely at Andrew's latest painting. Against a forlorn sky, a wizened crabapple clutched snow to its branches. Fermented berries lurked beneath, barely seen waxwings flocked to a drunken high. Zwiller shivered at the cold, heard tipsy twittering. He felt uncomfortable about something. Was it the light? The odd brush strokes? The flashes of...? What?

"It's, em, unusual."

Andrew ignored the attempted compliment. "Got a spot for it?"

"Of course." Zwiller was loyal even if sales were never much. "Or I might take it over to Ketchum."

Zwiller also represented Andrew in Sun Valley but found it difficult to place many works. Andrew wanted more sophisticated venues.

"Why not Seattle? San Francisco?"

"I've put out feelers. They're nervous." Zwiller twanged a rubber band, which slipped and shot into the air. "They admire your skill, but they don't understand what else is hiding there. I know you hear that a lot. Perhaps you should try more directness?"

Andrew always shrugged at this kind of remark. He was drawn to what lay beneath. The sky suggested shadowy raptors, invisible winds, high duststreams bearing seeds from Canada. Water roiled him to the bottom through layers of mocking light and startling thermoclines. Earth pulled him down through strata of soils, rocks, fossils and graves.

The more Andrew struggled to gain acceptance, the more his marriage faltered. Claire knew he was attempting to push far beyond the confines of the canvas, but she fast was losing sympathy.

The question of children, previously a small divide, was now a substantial chasm, broadening as Claire neared her forties. Years before, she'd forced the issue of testing. Doctors found no problems with either partner. Andrew, she decided, was somehow willing that there be no child.

They were in the kitchen, toying with herbal tea. Andrew's mind chased the sweet roots of Egyptian licorice into the dark sludge of the Nile, felt papyrus growing nearby, farmers toiling, scarabs rolling dung.

"Come back to earth, Andrew." Claire spoke gently, but he felt a hidden barb. He was startled by her smile. Often it reminded him of his mother's smile before the rafting accident. Today was different. Today Claire's smile contained, if not poison, bile.

"Would it hurt to be a bit more conventional?" she breathed a storm across the surface of her tea.

Beneath

"That's the one thing you should never ask of me."

"You can't push the public where it doesn't want to go."

"I have to try." Through the window he studied the striated bark of an old elm, sensed the insistent beetles underneath, the weakened sap struggling to rise. *Scarabs everywhere.*

A nationally-known critic came to Boise. Fitzpatrick Coe wanted to try Idaho's trout streams, and he knew how to fish his expense account. Coe gave Andrew's work a short mention in his column. He allowed the paintings a tiny hint of praise for technical skill, but put them down as 'less than fathomable.'

"Don't worry about it," Zwiller said. Coe's ad-filled magazine thunked into the waste basket. "People call him 'Glen' Coe, after the Scottish massacre. He ambushes artists and eats them for breakfast." Andrew laughed, but his eyes were stony.

That evening, Andrew needed to flee the studio. He proposed attending a new faculty exhibit. Claire excused herself. A board meeting. Andrew clambered into his least paint-spattered jeans, found a pair of socks, wet down his hair, set out alone.

The gallery reeked of adulation. A noisy crowd extolled Kim Carter's geometric collages and more of Tom Kaiser's big brown whirlpools.

Andrew limped about, daydreamed, dissected layers of conversation, music and street sounds. He heard asthmatic breathing, stomachs gurgling, the swish of nylon against thighs. He was standing bemusedly in front of a Kaiser painting when he sensed someone at his side.

"Well, look who's descended from the clouds." It was Kaiser himself, a flock of female fans in tow. "So, what do you think?"

Andrew gulped more cabernet. "You know what your favorite color is, Tom?" Kaiser raised an eyebrow in mild curiosity. "It's fawn. As in all that fawning."

Kaiser flinched, forced a smile, turned abruptly. His followers wheeled with him. Andrew raised his glass. "Go get 'em, Dr. K."

Andrew arrived home. No Claire. He sat in the dark kitchen, sipping peaty whisky and pondering his Scots heritage. A rough and tumble legacy, all kilts and claymores, but perhaps not quite justifying tonight's performance.

Claire finally came home, walked into the kitchen and turned on the light. When she saw Andrew, she blinked, laid down her purse.

Andrew told her what he'd said to Kaiser. "I'm not sure if I'm proud or embarrassed," he chuckled.

"Dammit, Andrew. You have to get along with them," Claire rummaged in a cupboard and found a box of animal crackers. She nibbled at a tiger. Andrew smelled Shalimar. Smoke. Booze. Something he couldn't quite place.

"Must have been a heckuva meeting," he said. Claire bit off a lion's head, stood there, crunching, staring.

Late one rainy fall afternoon, finding his studio refrigerator stinking of neglect, Andrew limped

Beneath

downstairs. He was thinking vaguely of food, but mostly pondering how to paint leaves while hinting at roots mutely touching others, suggesting the dying earth beneath. The kitchen was gloomy. He fumbled for the switch.

Where was Claire? Not at the counter, preparing reports, not curled in her favorite armchair, reading abstracts. The main floor was silent except for the tedious ticking of the grandfather clock and drips of water syncopating under a sink.

On the breakfast table, a yellow rose stood tall in a slender crystal vase. A handwritten note leaned against the glass.

A. - I'm sorry. Gone to chase my own dreams. Maybe to make babies if there's still time. "I love you" just isn't enough. Good luck. C.

Claire had used her best Fabriano stationery. He could see the soft watermark, below it the delicate whorls of rich pulp. The paper smelled faintly of bergamot, iris and vanilla. Andrew held the note closer to his face. Myrrh. A burst of wind and rain rattled the windows.

Andrew engaged a housekeeper and spent even more time in his studio. He repaired frames, prepared canvasses, tested colors. Stared into the foothills. Studied clouds and contrails.

His mind made another leap. Claire, James, Amelia Earhart. He rushed to work and painted a complex moment of transcendence. Silvered wings, yet nothing but sky. An emerald atoll, yet only empty sea. Abundant life, yet imminent death. Plunging and rising. Flying and drowning. Thriving corals, emboldened predators, deadly finery and camouflaged prey, turquoise descending into darkness. Loss, personal and universal.

'Amelia' spent three weeks in the gallery. Zwiller relayed the comments. People liked the colors but found the work confusing. A local critic said there was "too much perplexing subtext'. Someone wisecracked: "If that's Earhart, where's the plane?"

Andrew thrashed through a nightmare. He flung the canvas from a boat. Earhart, bleeding oils, disappeared under a heaving, unforgiving Pacific.

One gray and windy morning, leafless branches tattooing the eaves, wind chimes jangling in turmoil, Andrew clumped down to the kitchen. He needed something with a small point for an experiment with underlayers. As he reached for a toothpick canister, he was drawn to a newspaper the housekeeper had left on the counter.

An article described the discovery of the bones of England's Richard III, found below a parking garage. Richard had died over 500 years ago in the last battle of the Wars of the Roses. His mutilated body was buried in a monastery and soon forgotten. Later the monastery was razed, the site improperly mapped, the royal bones lost to the centuries.

Andrew studied the photo, transfixed. The grave rudely exposed, the melancholy, twisted skeleton, skull

Beneath

awry—embarrassment or plea, Andrew couldn't guess—spine achingly curved, ribs arching for air as though still protecting lungs, lank bones in fetal mimicry. Andrew smelled the dank concrete and slimy petrol, the wormy past, the rank and bloodied loam of the battlefield. He choked on the smug, lifeless dust of the monastery. Felt something fiercely pressing back against the crushing density of history. All that power. All that irreversible nothingness.

The fever of another idea staggered him. He hobbled upstairs, bellowing.

A painting! My kingdom for a painting!

He roared through reference materials, flung aside his books, slammed shut his computer and raced after his flying imagination.

Scat singing, he clamped a large gessoed canvas onto his biggest mahogany easel. He readied a palette, laid out brushes and knives. Looked. Feinted. Thrust. The first tiny daub was an angry ruby, tinged with mauve. Royal blood.

Bosworth Field. Andrew, in battle, staggered under the hoarse screaming din of death, gagged at howling blood and stink, winced as his horse and his tortured bowels gave way. Hissing arrows clanged his cuirass, snarled his cursing spine, piercing a weakness. A sword ripped his cheek, a halberd crashed, breached his skull, sliced life away, and blackness roared in with hell and damnation and then: rigorous centuries of waiting. Waiting for light, redemption, understanding.

The new painting bled over the canvas. The tumult, the fray, the dead, the dying, the fallen boar's head flag, the regicide, the tumbling crown.

Andrew stood back, regarding an epic both magnificent and horrible, with profound layers, physical and metaphysical. The toll of history. A drab future grave. A misunderstood monarch.

His eye fell on Claire's yellow rose, in the studio since the day she left. It leaned pitifully in the dusty crystal vase, a few limp petals awaiting a breath to release them.

Memento mori. Death lay under everything—roses, kingdoms, parents, marriages.

Death hid in the ambiguous layers of every one of his paintings. Death, sadness and guilt. The unholy trio. Under all life.

And there it was. Suddenly he knew what disturbed his audience. He knew what was missing. He knew he wasn't done with this painting.

First it needed to dry. He chided his impatience. He could stick it out for a few weeks. Richard had waited 500 years.

He hurled himself into paperwork. Limped around the neighborhood. Wrote long letters to Claire, tore them up. Watched the paint dry. *God, I'm living the metaphor.*

Two weeks. Three. It was time. Andrew prepared a new palette.

Taking a deep breath, he began painting directly on top of his bravura battle scene.

Bosworth Field disappeared. Over the slaughter, over the dying Richard, over the bloody transition of sovereignty, emerged a single elegant, enigmatic rose. Sensual, fiery. Gentle, caressing. The unusual stem twisted, curved awkwardly as though in pain, yet flaunted power and strength. Thorns threatened yet entreated, violated yet nourished. Fold upon creamy, equivocal fold dropped languorously toward a volcanic vanishing point.

The intricate blossom concealed Claire's farewell, the embattled Tudors, the cruel and loving twists of time. Rooted in the intensity of the secret masterpiece below, it spoke eloquently of beauty, of ambition. It told of power, loss. It entwined death with life and hope. The whole mysterious continuum.

For the first time in Andrew's work, there was a sense of redemption. *Death and guilt are hidden under everything. But renewal and transfiguration can exist there too.*

'Richard's Legacy' hung by itself on a main wall at the Zwiller. The curious hovered, stared, wondered, sipped their wine.

"Nicely-painted, if only a rose. Then, maybe..."

Some said they smelled the deep fragrance of an English country garden. Some sniffed, pronounced a darker, byzantine aroma. Some thought the painting strangely tormenting, but also oddly reassuring. Most felt a tremor of mortality.

Andrew, unnoticed, leaned against a side wall. Would anyone ever fully get his work? It didn't matter. He wondered if Claire would come by. He wasn't counting on it.

He thought of his life, the layers of difficulty, the challenges. He'd risen through it all, turned it into a singular artistic vision, now more balanced.

The secret didn't lie in achieving public understanding. It lay in understanding himself. It lay in knowing his voice was his own. Unique, strong, unconquerable.

Like his imagination.

He limped out of the shadows and stood in front of 'Richard's Legacy.'

He regarded it with a critical eye.

"Yes," said Andrew to himself. "Yes."

Acknowledgements

*The author appreciates the insights
and the encouragement he's received from*

Anthony Doerr
Kate Riley
Jonathan Phillips

Rodney Dotson
Mike Philley

Charles Palmer
Louis O. Girard

Susan Bono, *Tiny Lights*
The Wy Write group, Boise
The Idaho Writers Guild

About the Author

ERIC E. WALLACE writes fiction, poetry, plays and humor. His work has appeared in many periodicals, from *Alaska Magazine* to *Writers Digest,* in six print anthologies, and online at *WritersWeekly.com.*

His drama *Syd,* published in *Alaska Quarterly Review,* was performed throughout Alaska, in St. Ives, Cornwall, and, to critical acclaim, at the Edinburgh Fringe Festival in Scotland. His shorter plays have had staged readings in seven Pacific Northwest cities.

He lived for 25 years in Anchorage, Alaska, where he was an Emmy-winning public television writer-producer-director and air personality, a classical music host on public and commercial radio, and a humor columnist for the *Anchorage Times, Alaska Business Monthly* and *Alaska Bride and Groom.*

Eric is a roster member of the Idaho Writers Guild. He lives with his partner Kathy McGowan in Eagle, Idaho.

CPSIA information can be obtained at www.ICGtesting.com
Printed in the USA
BVOW07s1229050814

361643BV00002B/11/P